The

BALLAD

of

BIG

FEELING

The

BALLAD

of

BIG

FEELING

ARI BRAVERMAN

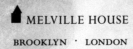

MELVILLE HOUSE

BROOKLYN · LONDON

The Ballad of Big Feeling
Copyright © Ari Braverman, 2019
All rights reserved
First Melville House Printing: July 2020

Melville House Publishing
46 John Street
Brooklyn, NY 11201
and
Melville House UK
Suite 2000
16/18 Woodford Road
London E7 0HA

mhpbooks.com
@melvillehouse

ISBN: 978-1-61219-767-8
ISBN: 978-1-61219-768-5 (eBook)

Library of Congress Control Number: 2020932926

Printed in the United States of America
1 3 5 7 9 10 8 6 4 2

A catalog record for this book
is available from the Library of Congress

for xxx

The

BALLAD

of

BIG

FEELING

I

A man's voice swells out from his chest and throat like a bubble, enveloping the first row of seats and expanding until it seems to fill the theater.

"She's having a seizure." Again, louder, with more urgency. "She's having a seizure!"

A girl slumps backward. Her head sinks awkwardly into her neck, jaw slack. But for her face, which is loose, it looks as though she's doing a dance in her seat. Her shoulders wiggle wildly. The Chinese logograms on her sweatshirt zigzag back and forth, up and down.

A woman sits by her left side, opposite the man whose voice has become so loud.

The woman forces herself to pull the girl close. In the blue light from the man's cell phone, the girl's cheeks and forehead are ragged with acne. The woman puts her hands around the girl's head, tilts it forward, and watches as saliva spools out of the girl's mouth onto their legs. There is no foam around her lips, and the woman thinks, That is just another cliché.

The woman's biceps ache, but the girl keeps vibrating. The woman's lover is there, somewhere to her left with a tub of popcorn in his lap, but now she is part of a new duo: the girl and her own self in an inadvertent posture of care.

In the darkness, the woman can feel a tide of attention turning toward them. The shouting man is on his feet. He wants to know—is anyone a doctor?

Another man strides up the aisle on long legs.

"I'm a neurologist," he says and steps into their row like a hero boarding a boat.

The movie has started. Discordant theme music fills the theater as the introductory credits roll.

The neurologist reaches across the woman's body to touch the girl. The woman watches his big watch snag some of the girl's hair while he thumbs back one eyelid and then the other. The doctor rubs his dry knuckles hard between the girl's tiny breasts and demands she return to consciousness. Her face and his hands flicker as different shades of green, blue, gold, and gray in the light from the screen.

"Young lady! Young lady! Young lady!"

People cluster around the row, dotting the aisles and leaning over each other. No one offers any suggestions, but the woman can hear them murmuring beneath the noise of the score.

Slowly, the girl rises out of her seizure. Her expression is one of mild disbelief, as though a stranger has just stepped very hard on her foot. She swivels her whole body from left to right to look around. The woman pulls her close, to keep her still, and tucks the hair behind her ears.

The doctor snaps his fingers in the girl's face.

"Where are your parents? Has this happened to you before? Young lady! Young lady! What is your name?"

But she cannot speak.

The houselights go up and the movie stops midscene. Onscreen the lead actor—a big star, the woman's favorite— is caught midspeech, his mouth puckered into a fleshy rosette. The woman wishes that this afternoon had not veered off on this trajectory.

Two young people come slowly through the aisles. Their movement is strangely subdued.

"Her English isn't very good yet," says the boy, who has almost no accent. "I'm her brother. This is my girlfriend. She didn't want to sit with us."

The girlfriend remains silent, her eyes fixed on the back wall.

"Do you want to switch places with me?" the woman says, very tired, unsure if she's addressing the doctor or the brother. The girl slumps against her, like they're two weasels in a dug-up nest. The bright lights hurt her eyes, so she shades the girl's face with her free hand.

"She looks pretty comfortable where she is," the doctor says, and people laugh. "You get seizures, too?"

The brother nods, smiling. The doctor continues.

"She's going to have one hell of a headache by the time you guys get to the hospital. Like the worst hangover in your life, right?"

Again, people laugh. The soundproofed walls make everyone sound flat, depthless. The woman would like to leave.

"Are you the mother?" says a person whose T-shirt reads TOO TIRED TO CARE.

"No," says the woman's lover. "Definitely not." His hand is hot and big on the back of her neck.

"My mom went to Taipei last year," the doctor says.

"You're not the mother?" says someone else.

"I thought she was with her."

"We're not."

"Do you have children?"

"No, we don't." The lover ventriloquizes so well, he even sounds a little indignant.

"The ambulance is here."

"You don't have any children?"

"I thought for sure she was the mother. I thought for sure you were the mother."

"No," the woman says finally. She and the girl and the lover are the only people still in their seats.

The loud man looks profoundly embarrassed. "But thank God for maternal instincts! She was way better about it than I was," he says and reaches forward to damply grasp the arm she has around the girl's body. "I'm glad you were here."

The lover is watching her with a strange expression.

The woman cannot find the words to say that everyone has the wrong idea. She cannot tell them she had come to the movies to escape responsibility and the unseasonable weather, and she cannot tell them that her lover being there is a mistake, that he had decided to come last minute, and that the popcorn and enormous soda belong only to him. She had wanted only the vacant feeling of being in a theater. She had been looking forward to this movie and she had been ready to watch, alone.

II

The woman enters a grocery store to do the shopping for herself and her old neighbor, who subsists on Social Security and decaf coffee with extra water. Her lover does his own shopping.

Every time she passes through the sensitive doorway she is strafed by a profusion of choice and a burst of air-conditioning. Overhead, white asbestos tiles form a second sky, and she blinks against its fluorescence. Everywhere she looks is packed with information.

She usually deals with this overload by buying the same items every two weeks: salad in a cellophane bag, sliced smoked turkey, whole wheat bread, store-brand cheddar cheese, peach-flavored individual yogurts, instant coffee, green apples, a six-pack of Diet Coke, and compunction in the form of skim milk.

She sometimes allows a concession for indulgence's sake— frozen chicken strips or frozen pizza, for example—and will tuck into it only when she is at home by herself, or when her lover is sound asleep on late nights and she has been awake for hours, when convenience feels like shelter.

Everything she buys herself must either be microwavable or edible raw because the woman does not know how to cook and cannot fathom how other people learn. As with any improvable talent, she believes the capacity is mostly genetic. When she watches her lover cook for them, it is like watching an alchemical preparation.

After too much deliberation, she selects a basket in which someone has left their shopping list. The woman picks it up. The handwriting forms a matrix:

sherry flank steak whipping cream
poblano anise radicchio sundried tom.

Everything about the list speaks to self-assuredness—its organization, the precision of each handwritten character, and especially the ingredients themselves. Probably none of them are on sale.

Powered by rumination, the woman wheels her cart through the aisles.

She collects her own items but also looks for the others on the list. She finds the radicchio among the leafy greens and picks one up. The little vegetable is bouncy and firm, asking to be patted, and she cradles it in her hands before reluctantly putting it back.

She finds the poblano, too, with its dolphin's skin; the steak, presliced and fanned out like an array of tongues on

Styrofoam; the tomatoes in their thick jar. Everything seems so friendly, welcoming her into a fraternity of health and good taste with their rawness, their demand for transformation. She could never place these items in her own basket.

She imagines the radicchio in a bowl on a clean table. Someone she cannot see has sliced it in half, and a television flickers comfortingly in the background. This meal, she knows, will be a light evening supper comprised of many small portions.

Slowly, the rest of the house coalesces. The living room is red like the steak, and like a womb, and like a throat. There is a garden, and all the windows are open to catch the sound of the leaves, which, at night, might whisper the woman's name in the dark.

Holding this abstract totem in her mind fills the woman with secondhand peace in the vivisecting space of the grocery store. She becomes a happy tourist and then something more—an expatriate from life.

She tries to imagine the author of the list but cannot. She can only think of the detritus they might leave behind: keys and open mail on the table, a purse or a money clip on a low bench near the front door. The sound of jewelry on a tabletop at the end of a long day. The warmth of their body on the toilet seat, a smear of peanut butter or lipstick on the rim of a water glass.

The woman follows their specter from room to room through the liquid floor plan. The floors are blond, the ceilings high and rounded out with shadow.

The woman passes a fresh bundle of cut flowers on the sideboard in the hall. Sweet pea blossoms, ranunculus, hollyhock, dahlia . . . she has never bought flowers before, for any occasion or any person, and lingers on this image, turning it over in her mind as she would a blossom in her palm, inspecting it from every angle and possibility.

The woman imagines herself emerging from this home every morning, drawn from its substance and not the sentimentality of human intercourse. She would have been a friendly baby, a precocious child, a droll teenager with many admirers, and, finally, an early success.

III

When the siren goes off, the woman is in the street between her car and the sidewalk, holding her neighbor's groceries. It is a long, brassy sound but contains something, too, of the shofar. Her golden tooth is singing and she touches it with her tongue, imagining that the sound of the siren is hurting her, though of course there are no nerves left in the pulp.

Once, in childhood, she was home alone during a tornado touchdown. The siren had sounded exactly the same as this one does now. She took herself to the house across the street, rang the doorbell, and joined a family of strangers in their basement.

Listening to the siren now, the woman realizes she is not surprised. She has anticipated violence her entire life. She believes everyone expects it. That it exists as a hysterical undercurrent beneath every conversation. Fear itches her skin, and she lets the bags slip from her wet hands to the ground. It is a good, clear day—there is no weather to blame.

"What's going on?" she says to her neighbor, who has been waiting on the porch with a cigarette.

The old woman cups her hand around her ear and, squinting through smoke, shakes her head.

"The siren. Do you know what's happening?" The woman gestures as she speaks, circling the air above her head with a raised arm and a pointer finger. The siren ends as she pronounces the final syllable, and her voice, pitched higher with tension, clatters around on the empty street.

"It's Wednesday," says the neighbor, opening the door to the shabby bungalow.

It is the kind of property the woman's mother would have bought at auction many years ago. The siding is missing in several important places, and inside, nicotine stains all of the walls and ceilings.

The neighbor has decorated it like a real country house. Hand-stitched quilts cover much of the furniture and some of the walls, electric hurricane lamps illuminate nooks and table tops. The sofa, draped with various skins and blankets, smells faintly of urine when the woman sits on it. She leans forward to rest her elbows on her knees and indexes the neighbor's belongings: a painting of the American flag with only forty-eight stars; a Rolodex on the coffee table, sticky with old smoke; bunny ears on the TV set, wrapped in foil. All of it a reminder of the incredible, inconvenient length of a human life.

"When you were out there with your mouth hanging open you looked like you were about seven years old," yells the neighbor as the screen door bashes behind her. "Will you look at something for me?" She shuffles forward and hitches up her T-shirt. She turns around to offer the woman her tiny back, which might be a child's back it is so smooth and so small and so devoid of muscle. "Do you see anything? If I have shingles I'll kill myself." Her yellow fingers fan out along her little rib cage to indicate a spot they can't quite reach. The woman touches it. She has always been afraid of the bodies of old people.

"No, you look good. Maybe skinny. A little dry."

"Thank you, dear. Time for coffee, but first: the john." She disappears into the house's deep interior, where the woman has never been. The toilet flushes and runs, the microwave hums because the neighbor hates waiting on the kettle.

Eventually she comes back carrying an enamel butcher's tray. The coffee is Folgers and the old neighbor likes it diluted. When she sips her new dentures clack reassuringly against the rim of the mug.

"The city tests the sirens every Wednesday before lunch," she says, slowly setting her body down into a scuffed leather armchair.

There is much kindness in this explanation. The woman knows her neighbor regards her with equal amounts of tenderness and exasperation.

"I've never heard one before," says the woman, partly as a talking point and partly to regain her dignity, settling back among the skins. Outside, the world shuffles itself back into place.

"Well you're usually at work on Wednesdays, aren't you?"

"I guess that's right." Today, the woman has stayed home to show the landlord where termites have built up their mud tubes around the old foundation.

"There you go. Jumpy, jumpy!" says the old neighbor, struggling up to use the toilet one more time.

IV

"Anyway, he just slipped out of me," her cousin—a new mother—continued over the phone. "It took forty-five minutes. The placenta came an hour later."

The woman had always thought of the placenta as a thin membrane, like a plastic bag. She learned recently it's actually a whole organ, but she still can't remember the different stages of labor.

"That's unbelievable," she said, unsure if she had chosen the correct adjective. "I'll come as soon as I can."

"You don't have to do that."

"I have to see my mom anyway."

There is a pause—the woman thinks, A postpartum pause, not a pregnant one!—and the stupidity of her own sense of humor nearly makes her laugh. But of course, she doesn't. This is a serious moment.

"I haven't been over to see her lately. We've just been so busy." The cousin's voice is telling. Isn't she so sorry? "How is she feeling?"

"I don't know."

Weeks later the woman sits in the back seat of her cousin's car, crossing a lake at sixty-six miles per hour. The speed
limit is seventy; the new father is driving. The woman is alert
for any change in her cousin—a sudden inner voluptuousness
or docility—that might indicate she has become a different
person.

Below them the water changes colors with the sky as the
sun plunges toward the lake. The baby sleeps in his car seat
with his lips puckered in the inverse shape of a nipple. The
woman cannot help but imagine his little body in the event
of a collision, spiraling through the air, his pale blanket flung
out like a cape.

"Do you ever ride with him in your arms?"

"Oh no! Never!" The cousin laughs. She has turned around
in her seat to talk, and the woman finds comfort in the
chicken pox scars on her nose and forehead. Her broad face
still reminds the woman of a clean dish.

And yet the cousin's body is different. It had once been
so sleek and firm, perfect for athletics (that build runs in the
family; the woman's mother has it, too), and had made the
woman jealous for years.

In person, the tits of first-time motherhood are tremen-
dous. The woman tries to locate the feeling of having a womb,
but cannot. It is easier for her to pretend to remember having
been contained by one, despite its chemical shortcomings and
the truncated duration of her stay.

And there it is, the purpose of her visit, which has become
a constant flickering around the woman's brain stem.

Her mother is sick.

Soon their house will belong to a family of strange strangers.

"Well, thanks for picking me up. I guess my dad is out of town."

"Thank you for coming."

It is nighttime when they enter the subdivision. The cousin and her husband own their place because he has a good job with the real estate development company. Walking into the big blue house, the woman feels flayed down to her marrow. She might just fly apart. Immaculate textiles abound. Abundance glows from every surface. Even the potted plants look like they have self-esteem. Out back, framed by French doors, the lawn unfurls beneath a floodlight. Red clouds racing above the ornamental trees mean rain—a cozy proposition, combined with the ceiling fan and the lull of the suburbs. Back home, the woman only rents a small house on a cul-de-sac with her lover.

"How did you figure out how to do all this?" As she speaks, the woman's mouth tastes like salt. Travel must have made her very tired. It has been so long since she and her cousin have seen each other. Childhood flickers inside the woman's brain as a series of shared baths and breakfasts. But here is her cousin now, in life, a tall stranger with forty extra pounds and a productive sex life.

"She's been nesting," the husband says and touches his wife on her hip. For the first time the woman regrets this leg of her visit.

"Do you want to hold him?"

The woman nods silently and accepts the infant into her

arms. He wiggles and sighs. "This is a little scary," she says. The woman neither enjoys nor dislikes his odor, though it does conjure an image: a wheat field warming in the sun.

Every time she holds a baby, or speaks to someone about their own children, the limits of the woman's frame of reference lurch into view. She is always just talking about herself.

"I can't believe anybody is ever this small."

"You're doing a great job."

The praise feels good, like a dribble of warm liquid. She wants to travel back in time and size, to shrink, to climb inside her cousin, come out again, and grow up differently.

"Really?"

But proof: the baby boy slips into sleep.

The rain arrives as a rollicking storm.

After dinner and drinks the woman does the dishes and joins the new father for television. His wife has gone to take her first shower in six days. In the recliner to the left, he looks like a small boy bedraggled by a long day. He can barely keep his eyes open. The woman has a white blanket tucked around her legs, and a surge of contentment makes her generous.

"Go to bed. I'll watch him until she comes back." She flaps her hands at the plastic bassinet that contains his son. Thunder shakes the windowpanes but, nestled in blankets, softer than his tiny pillow, the baby sleeps on.

"It's so good of you to be here," says the new father. "Family means a lot to her. And I'm sorry your man couldn't come. It's been a minute since we've seen you both." He swallows the final word with another yawn, and the woman stares into his gullet.

"See you tomorrow," she says.

Alone, the woman goes to the refrigerator and retrieves another beer, hidden behind many pouches of breast milk. She settles back on the couch and balances the clicker on her knee. When she changes the channel the baby wakes up. Before she remembers he's too young to see, she believes he is looking at her.

"Hey," she says. He whimpers, and as she lifts him from his bedding, his head flops backward. He wails. A little drunk, fearing rebuke, the woman takes him outside.

There are fewer mosquitoes than usual because of the rain. Darkness and water mass beyond the pale plane of the porch. She can't see the flagstone walk or the locust trees. Thinking of a warm sack of grain, she holds the baby a little tighter. He has stopped crying to listen to the rain. He is three weeks old. Two cats—a tabby and a black—creep out from behind the woodpile and slide themselves around her ankles. They want food. The baby wants food. His little mouth smacks open and closed. He gazes toward her face, vulnerable and benevolent at the same time. In the nighttime his eyebrows are invisible.

"There's nothing for you in these tits," the woman says and inserts her pinky between his gums. His sucking pulls the blood into her fingertip, and she tries to remember that, for now, he is just a small animal.

V

"You love me so much, you can hardly stand it," says the mother, who is also a monolith, toppling. Her body is long and broad, and her female child has a difficult time looking at it directly. Instead she looks at the microwave, which blinks in a way that seems both friendly and aggressive.

It is ten o'clock in the morning, and the child is nine years old.

"If I died, you wouldn't even know what to do with yourself," the mother says. She pokes her child in the belly and laughs. "You pretend like you don't like me, but you like me."

The child betrays herself by smiling. The mother's body is fragrant. Sweat mats the hair at her temples. She has already been up for hours, working on the house, picking at a long scab on her forearm where a nail scratched her while she was gutting the attic.

There had been many dead squirrels and a jar of red marbles.

"Can I have it?" the child had said.

"You just want everything, don't you?" said her mother.

This morning the child has just finished her bowl of instant mashed potatoes. An unopened box of trisodium phosphate sits on the floor by her chair, and she places her feet on top of it. The red and yellow packaging looks bright but not cheerful.

"I'd really like it if you could do something besides sit around all day today," the mother says, rising from the table with the dirty bowl in one hand and a coffee cup in the other. Purpose—of the room, the gutted house, the child—gathers at her shoulders and trails like a cape. "You probably could use some exercise."

"Okay," the child says.

"Why don't you ask if there's anything you can do to help me out today?"

"Is there anything I can do to help out today?" The child pictures a series of different keys being tried in the same lock before one clicks in.

They march together through their small backyard to stand beside a mound of dirty insulation. The mother tucks the child's sleeves into a pair of gloves that are too big, does the same with her socks, a paper mask, and a pair of sweatpants.

Light bounces off dirt and pavement and brick into the child's face.

The mother points from the pile to the alley and says, "Put that in that." Beyond the low brick wall there's the dumpster and a transformer humming above it.

"It's really hot," the child says, and her voice fills her with shame.

She is afraid of the alley, like she is afraid of the nicotine stains on the ceiling in her bedroom and the boiler when it clicks on at night.

Sweat drips down her spine and into the split between her cheeks.

"Then you'll have to chop-chop."

For a long time the child cannot move. She stands, smelling her own breath inside the paper mask, even after the mother's car whines out of the driveway and down the street. Wasps and black flies buzz among the cat shit and rotten fruit hidden in the high grass.

But the mound does disappear, one small handful at a time.

As she works, the child watches from the corner of her eye for any car or stranger, until the phone rings and she goes to answer it.

"I'm calling because I forgot to tell you how much I love you," the mother says.

The child presses the receiver against her face and moves as close to the window as the cord will allow. Sparkling fibers cover her arms and belly.

"Don't you have anything to say?"

The mother's voice clots with need, but the child cannot speak. Itchiness burrows into her skin until she gags. She drops the phone into the sink and fumbles at her pants, the gloves, her socks, and underwear. The child is naked in the kitchen, scratching hard enough to hurt, staring out, scratching harder, staring through the window at a little plum tree burdened with fruit.

VI

Yes, she loves being kissed so often and with so much tongue, she tells her lover in the early morning.

Yes, she wants, enjoys, and appreciates the packaged cornbread that always comes with her coffee, she tells the cashier in the later morning.

No, she doesn't want American cheese on her sandwich— she doesn't like it, either, she tells her coworker around noon.

Yes, she loves the feeling of central air on such a hot day, she tells her boss in the early afternoon.

Yes, she is tired but fulfilled after such a long week, she tells her neighbor in the early evening.

VII

Even now, beyond the weight gain and acid reflux of her childhood, the woman cannot square the perverse combination of her fast, skittish brain with the short, soft body it lives inside.

She drives to the gym and parks in the lot. The strip mall facade radiates heat from its bank of mirrored windows, and the woman does not want to see the reflection of her face moving as she talks.

"I pay to come here," she says, wincing at the silliness of talking to a seat belt, some upholstery, and an empty cupholder as though they comprise an audience. "Human beings are stupid," she says, kills the ignition, and goes inside.

She likes this gym because some of its employees are fat and all of them are unobtrusive. Yes, several patrons have bodies that look better—harder, more controlled—than hers, but overall the atmosphere lends itself to the convivial ugliness of hard work. And the woman appreciates how easy it is to compartmentalize her time here.

GET IN GET OUT, goes the promotional poster.

Recently she switched from the StairMaster to the track

because a magazine article claimed running would help her develop lean muscle. The woman wants to look more like a knife, less like several dollops of cream.

At first, even after her stretches, the woman's body jounces uncomfortably as it absorbs the shock of each step.

Ten minutes later, her seventh lap is almost complete. Endorphins unspool in her brain. The woman overtakes someone shorter and thicker than she is. His round bottom wags and his elbows slice through the air in time with his steps.

"On your left!" The woman surges forward feeling as free as a stupid young man. She could ask him for a high five.

Her muscle memory twitches alive. Humans have always needed to exercise their bodies, and it is good that she no longer exempts herself from this community.

Afterward, in the locker room, she showers and goes to look at herself in the mirror. Her thighs and ass could almost be the haunches of a powerful animal, of a pit bull or a lion or a horse. She stamps her leg once, twice, and watches it shudder biologically. She takes a photo and sends it to her lover who will respond, sweetly, as though the image titillates him. And maybe it will. She slips on her shirt, tucking her phone into a top pocket.

Some of the ceiling lights have burned out, giving this section of the locker room the ambiance of an enchanted glade. An oracular voice drifts from an invisible corner.

"You shouldn't keep your cell phone near your breasts, especially since they're so big."

Blinking with embarrassment, the woman turns toward

the sound. It belongs to a thin woman perched cross-legged on the bench. Her back is very straight and her athletic wear does not cut into her flesh. She holds a reusable cup with a screw-on top. There is something brown and thick inside it.

The woman cannot figure out if she should first cover herself or reply. The back of her head pulses with dismay—she hadn't known anybody else ever used her favorite bay of lockers.

Finally she locates and deploys her most useful phrase.

"I'm sorry?"

"I'm talking about cancer," says the stranger. She sips her drink. She is much thinner than the woman, and much older. "Phones radiate. Don't you have a purse or a back pocket?" A familiar thing lives inside this person—a feral intensity, peering out, burning through calories and relationships. "You come every week?"

"I do." The woman is cowed and jealous. Beneath the stranger's appraisal, the woman feels her body softening, opening itself for input.

"I come here to use the weight machines but I only run outside. You might consider doing the same thing; it's much better for you and it could help your gait," says the hard stranger, pausing again to suck a glob of smoothie. The woman watches her stringy throat move up and down as she swallows. She reminds the woman of a collapsed star.

"What's wrong with my gait?" She glances at the mirror once more and sees that the haunches have disappeared, replaced by the dappled thighs of a modern worker.

"You're just the littlest bit knock-kneed," says the hard stranger. "Do you ever think about running outside?"

What an impossible scenario! The woman would like to light herself on fire and leave behind only her skeleton and the echo of a pithy response.

"I've thought about it," she says, which is true. She decided months ago that she could never withstand the smell of cut grass or the bright light or the civilians watching her struggle over topography. "Really, though, I have somewhere to go." The woman hurries into her shorts.

"I'm trying to be helpful," the hard person says placidly. She takes another sip and makes no move to stand.

The woman shifts her weight from one foot to the other. Stuck to her spot, she cannot figure out what to do. If she turns to leave, the hard stranger will see all the wobble inside her shorts.

But her legs leap into their own animal life. They scissor vigorously—back and forth, together and apart—and the woman is off, past the drinking fountain and its bacteria colonies, past the treadmills and their swinging ponytails, through the revolving door, and into the heat of the car beside the empty passenger's seat. It is the best role model. The seat has neither hardness nor wobble. But only the bare whiff of spirit she assigns it.

VIII

"You better pick it up if she shits," says the man with half his face in a beard and the other half shaded by the sprawling live oak. He is lying on his side on a mattress, and the woman realizes that she is standing in his bedroom.

For a long time, the woman has suspected that this city—the city of her adulthood, a thousand miles away from anything familial—might be a place suited only to the very young, the very rich, or the very drunk. It is a wild and difficult place and the biggest city she's ever lived in. Light and heat and the visual density of long grass and blighted mansions press down, always.

At first it felt close to her fantasy of living in a dead city. She resents her favorite book from adolescence, with its apocalyptic vistas and punky hairdos and sexy horseback. Its counterpart—this place—is not very romantic. There are potholes everywhere and parking is bad. She has friends missing teeth. She herself has let another good tooth go bad, as though it were nothing more than a forgotten piece of fruit.

They are all part of this place, which is so different from

the place of her childhood, with its yellowness, its spacious-
ness, its sporadic hills and rich soil. This place is green and
black and pink, overlaid with a golden sheen that is not yellow,
and is encased in a permanent darkness. The population tends
toward politeness and slowness and cruelty.

Appalled, delighted, the woman realizes for the millionth
time that she lives here and not there.

"I'm sorry if she's bothering you," she says, and calls the
dog, who will not listen.

"She's not bothering me. I just don't want to smell shit all
day is what I'm saying."

"Of course not." The woman feels for her crown with her
tongue because she'd like to occupy her mouth with something that isn't language.

Both the woman and this bearded man are in the park
with their lovers: she can see a woman, very tan and very
thin, soaking a piece of clothing in the fountain water. Her
own lover stands near the entrance to the park, speaking to
his parents on the telephone, pacing through the high grass. It
is a Saturday. She can see that he is laughing and listening, so
handsome and good. He is like a photograph—his core com-
position will never change, though she knows that with time
his edges will soften and blur.

"Is that your boyfriend?"

"It is."

"He looks like he's talking to his mother."

The woman does not marvel at the bearded man's guess,
or at the intimacy he has fostered with her in only a few seconds. The day beats in this moment between them, making a

meaningful frieze of the heat and the smell of his filthy body and the alien smoothness of her gold cap against her tongue.

"I think he is."

The man reclines into his original position on his back, with one arm pressed casually against his eyes. The woman can see the inside of his thin arm, the flesh of which is less brown than the rest of him. It looks very soft.

There are parakeets in the top branches overhead, as foreign as sparrows and, unshackled from the domesticity of their forbearers, even wilder.

"They're parakeets," says the man who lives in the park.

"Yes, I know," says the woman.

"I saw a bunch of them eating a dead crow once," the man says. "Now that was disturbing." The man folds both arms behind his head and looks dreamily up through the leaves. The woman could almost go and sit next to him and reach forward to play with her toes. The urge to make conversation overcomes her.

"That's basically cannibalism," she says, and together they laugh.

IX

"That's the little girl who lives next door," says the old neighbor from her new special bed in the living room. The opposite of a baby, she has just come home from the hospital and is on some funny drugs. She is still strong and bad-tempered enough to have kicked off her blankets. Her short thighs shine in the light from the picture window opposite her bed, and the woman can see her pubis; she has almost no body hair.

"She looks grown up enough to me," says the neighbor's daughter as she covers her mother back up. Her movements are studied, patient. This scene is so intimate that the woman must avert her eyes and doesn't mind being spoken about as though she were another object in the room.

The Rolodex is still on the arm of the couch where she left it. In this new time of personal emergency, the air in the room has adopted a special shine. If it were a person it would be smiling sadly. Maybe waving.

Apart from the hospital bed, the only new addition is a dialysis machine atop a dresser in the corner. The smell that the woman had always thought came from a charming incontinence, it turns out, is really from kidney disease. There is often ammonia on the old neighbor's breath. In their year of knowing each other, the woman has gone from a yard waver to a grocery getter to a concern haver.

"I'll get you some water," the woman says loudly.

The kitchen is shrouded in its usual darkness, but the compost smell is gone. The garbage has been taken out. The woman opens the refrigerator and finds several cans of sugarless, geriatric meal replacement, some spinach, and a small cluster of broccoli. Someone has taken away all the lunch meat and fruit juice cocktail. Someone has put an open box of baking soda on the top shelf and replaced the bar soap with a plastic bottle of dishwashing liquid.

The woman thinks that there are times when she would like to be ill and have someone take good care of her. She follows the thread of this thought back to where it spools around the old neighbor looking tired, looking young, looking old, and her daughter timelessly servile at the head of the bed.

"The kitchen looks great," she says to her neighbor as she places the glass on the bed's precarious tray. "I'm jealous!"

"I think she'd probably trade places with you in a second," says the daughter, adjusting her mother's pillows.

"I wouldn't! She's mad at her own shadow," says the old neighbor from her nest.

"I don't think that's how the saying goes, Mom."

"I didn't say it was. That's too high. You'll kill my neck if you leave it like that."

As she fusses, the daughter's body moves in and out of the light from the picture window, and the woman can see that she has eczema in the crooks of both elbows and on her cheek. Reflexively, the woman scratches these spots on her own body.

The old neighbor reclines like an icon and closes her eyes. The daughter, an attendant in the bondage of love, curls her brown arm in the air over her mother's head, a half inch from the nimbus of gray hair. Their bodies in the shadowed room make a fresco that speaks to the tenderest lessons of every religion.

The woman is sure that she will die before this neighbor does. The neighbor who, according to the woman's limited understanding, has never not lived on this street, and who will legislate its character in perpetuity.

The woman and the neighbor's daughter try to make conversation while they wait for the old neighbor to get sleepy and go to sleep. Why is sleeping always the goal of recuperation, the woman thinks, aware that her companion might not appreciate the question.

"It's been nice to meet you," she says, and her voice is very loud in the slumber room. It arcs over the bed, raining down the guileless, brutal energy of good health.

Instead of, "Shut the fuck up," the daughter says, "Let's let her rest."

Together they go out to stand on the porch and look out at the world that surrounds the neighbor's shabby bungalow. In almost every yard, monstera leaves boast their hugeness and vitality. A crow retrieves a piece of bright trash from the gutter and flies off into a nearby tree.

"The other day someone told me he saw a bunch of parakeets eating a dead crow, once," says the woman, her voice unnaturally loud now that they have left the somnambulant air of the house. The daughter puts one of her mother's cigarettes in her mouth and laughs politely around it.

"I don't even smoke," she says, and something like fury trembles her voice. She scratches the plaque on her face with red fingernails. "I tell her to quit every time we talk. I don't know why I do that. I guess I can't help it." Her nails click as she lights the cigarette and then offers up the pack as if by reflex. The woman takes one, though she does not smoke either, and leans toward the proffered flame.

The woman indicates her little house, kitty-corner across the street where it is looking so cute today: the landlord has finally had the grass cut. The white siding catches sun and shadow in a very flattering way. Hopefully the neighbor's daughter will get the right idea—that the materials of the woman's life are all optimistic and everyone has so much to look forward to.

X

The woman's friend is smart. She thinks often about what regular people do and don't deserve.

"I know someone, a modern Maoist, who actually believes in the radical potential of luxury," said this friend, her voice tolling from inside her fantastic neck—it is the neck of a horse or a beautiful dog. Lean and firm and well-tendoned.

The woman had not had the emotional muscle to say that she didn't care about radical luxury. The woman is solvent. She has had her job—her fine job, her OK job—for a while now, and it's not going anywhere. She wants to soothe herself with a beautiful object, and so today she will buy some shoes.

The store is small and filled with expensive inventory. The woman has been here before but only to look around. Next door is a small perfume shop named after a piece of arcane mythology. Maybe she will go there after making this purchase. A long time ago, before the health problems that are also money problems, but after the lessons about God and violence, her mother taught her about oud and civet: "Unless you look like a model or a movie star, it matters what you wear and how you smell."

The woman likes to dress her body well whenever she emerges from the shell of her house into public. In her house clothes, she likes to sit with her hand on her belly or between her legs, idly masturbating on the couch, feeling how long it's been since she did any sit-ups or groomed her pubic hair, or how long it will be until she menstruates again. But outside, she doesn't experiment. She knows the shapes that draw attention to the long bones in her face and chest.

When the woman enters the store, a little chorus of brass bells announces her arrival. The homey sound feels incongruous compared with the woman's experience of contemporary life, but then again this is the kind of place that sells a feeling of repose in an age in which so many things are fast and intangible.

Somewhere beyond the parking lot, the city, and even farther away, across many state borders, is her hometown. She cannot remember how she arrived here. There have been many vectors leading up to this moment, so many strings tying it all up, but she cannot see or feel them.

"This pair of mules from the front window," she says disjointedly. Somehow she's holding the store model up but does not remember taking it out of the display. The left shoe minus its mate, looking a little funny. She thinks, It might as well be me.

It is olive green. The heel is prominent but not overwhelming, about an inch-and-a-half tall. Mules. The name is so funny and perfect. On one hand, like the animal, they are

hybrid—half open, half closed. On the other, they are completely impractical, totally unsuitable for any kind of labor or
physical performance.

"In olive, please," she says. The woman's tone reveals
that she is different from her usual child-minded self. Is it
the anticipation of a money exchange doing this? No—she
has always been adjacent to money, in some form or another,
though her mother has finally made herself poor.

While she waits for the young man to return with her
selection, the woman moves among the display tables and
expands. She feels like she's entered a different decade. Like
she could be smoking inside and solving the country's problems with a little preemptive thought. A thread of mania
worms its way from her heart to her lungs, then up into her
throat. Her voice will reveal it. She is a grand gesture, the size
of a skyscraper.

She is still holding the lone shoe. She feels its supple crafts-
manship. These are the most expensive shoes she's ever
asked to try on and she has decided that she will buy them,
regardless.

The young man is now kneeling at her feet. He is fitting
her left foot into the measuring device with its angular toggle.
The metal feels cold.

"You're almost a half size," he says. "We don't have these in
a half size. If you really want them, you'll have to go down a
size and get them stretched."

"Originally, mules were meant only for the boudoir," she
says so that the young man can enjoy the exquisiteness of her
sense of humor.

He is meant to laugh but says nothing, makes no murmur of acknowledgment. She is looking down at the top of his head and at the nape of his neck and thinking how easy it would be to kill him, if she decided that was something she wanted to do.

XI

"Say girl, I enjoy them new shoes," says the woman's strong friend, shouting because the truck's windows are down and a loud highway wind fills the cab and because he is exuberantly, ebulliently male.

The hot city, sliced in half by the overpass, spreads out beneath them in a disappointing carpet. The overpass is halfway as a high as the tallest business tower. If the building were closer, the woman could look inside and see people working through their weekends.

"You could never afford them," she says, fulfilling her role in their routine: the hillbilly and the Jew. The bone and the brain.

"I'm taking you for a proper American breakfast. Don't tell your rabbi."

Their dynamic has become so customary the woman can no longer tell if she likes it or not.

The strong, male friend exits onto a cloverleaf but stops halfway down, where a foreign coupe blocks the lane. Somehow its undercarriage has caught the curb on the passenger's side, just in front of the rear wheel. The driver must have lost control for a moment, or stopped paying attention and then, whoops, over and up and stuck.

The car must have once been beautiful. Now it's in bad shape, and the woman can tell it's filled with trash.

"He needs a push."

"I'm not good at that," the woman says and, though his profile is black against the window, she can feel her friend's dirty look. He was an athlete once. He works construction. He has been a man for his whole life, surrounded by a climate of physical confidence. They have never been lovers, but she once wanted him very badly. His competence entranced her. She liked it when he patted the top of her head, when he was a big brother. She liked his condescension and his knowing. She liked his height and bulk and fair complexion. She liked that he grew up tinkering with objects. She liked his appreciation of himself and his investment in the various projects he started and always finished—she liked his integrity, which had turned out not to be contagious.

She had not anticipated that their friendship would outlast the length of her infatuation, but here they are, old enough that red fur has sprouted across his shoulders, arms, and hands, and old enough that her desire has, mostly, turned into something else.

They park behind the coupe and disembark. A heavy man stands next to it with his hands on his head. The woman feels very vulnerable because there is no sidewalk.

"Need some help, brother?" says her friend.

"I can steer," the woman says, hating the sound of her own voice.

"Who is this? Your wife?" The driver's head glistens. "Nobody drives this car but me," he says. His shoes, like hers, are impractical—sandals with thick, dingy socks, in spite of the season. The woman is nervous. She does not want to touch him or smell his body and must resist the urge to hold her breath. She is too hot to ask any meaningful questions.

"Let's get," says her friend, clapping the man's dense shoulder. In doing so, this friend becomes even more of a man. The woman knows: this change is minute but important. "She can earn her bacon."

Behind them traffic curves back toward the interstate. No one honks and no one offers to help. Two people stare from inside a black sedan and, embarrassed, the woman takes her place at the bumper beside her friend. The driver eases himself behind the steering wheel and when he turns the engine over exhaust blows against her legs.

Her friend says, "Suck in your gut," counts to three, and they push. Unfamiliar fibers twitch inside the woman's thighs and biceps as she bears forward, willing the coupe to budge. Her feet slide around inside her new mules and she grips the insoles with her toes. A new blister is teaching her that the shoes, heartbreakingly, are too small.

The family lore goes back as far as she can remember: Everyone on your father's side has a weak back—especially your father and especially you.

And the woman knows that she must not continue. The

sun has filled up her head, burned off all the clouds, and now nothing shields them from the peeled sky. She needs a break. She steps down off the curb and puts one swollen hand against her throat.

A teacher once said she had a mind like a combustion engine.

"Help me, goddammit!"

"I'm not good at this," she says, aware of how her limbs protrude from her trunk. "I'm sorry." Her voice wavers with contrition.

Power seems to vibrate from his big body into the bumper. She has never seen someone produce so much sweat so fast. It runs down his calves and into his dusty boots. The hair on his knuckles is wet. His back is almost horizontal with effort, and the woman imagines the tightness in his neck and belly and rectum. He has become something primeval, like a forest or a herd of red cattle, seen from a distance.

In a separate universe, the driver revs his engine. The car rocks forward and back and forward again. Metal grinds against the concrete and the sound hurts the woman's teeth. Her friend minces forward with his heels off the ground. His face resembles a shiny, peaceful mask, but his arms are shaking. Otherwise his work is invisible.

Suddenly the car slips free. A simple change in its status: up to down, stuck to unstuck. The young woman's friend is soaked and gasping. His nipples and belly protrude through his wet T-shirt. The driver honks wildly, waving his thanks in the rearview mirror, and the coupe drifts down the ramp into a dead neighborhood.

Back in the truck, the woman hands over her water bottle and with it a small redress. Her friend swigs three times and gives it back, returning clemency. His smell fills the cab—a combination of onions and warm hair. She puts her mouth over the spot where he has left the most saliva and it tastes so good.

XII

The girl pretends the whole town is dead. She is too old for games like this one, but she indulges herself anyway, dangling her legs from a low structural wall outside her mother's house. Sunlight moves across her knees. Her eyes and scalp itch with hay fever. She's been eating too much dairy and her guts don't feel well.

In her fantasy, life turns predatory and meaningful. The country's population has almost disappeared but buildings and infrastructure remain, jutting from the landscape like the bones of a carcass. She says, nearly in prayer, "This is the future." An annulment of time. There are no other countries. There is a yellow star but no sun, a white rock in the night sky but no moon. No evolution, no smart, no stupid, no college, no virginity, no cell phone, no money. Strange, windy new gods blow in and she announces their names from the highest empty skyscraper. Scraps flicker along the empty streets. Wild dogs hunt in the streets and sometimes she feeds on the scraps they leave behind. She has no family and no friends. Without them she moves only according to need, devoid of expectation, just a shape among shapes. Her body hardens with muscle and instinct. She imagines herself with a boy's long back and long hair. A flat chest.

But in real life her breasts, already pendulous, stretch marked, are growing larger. She is smart and overweight. She gets out of breath going up a flight of stairs. Friends have lately taught her to smoke cigarettes and drink gin out of a plastic bottle. She has never touched anyone else's privates. Sometimes, at night, she frightens herself into hearing her own name when her mother isn't home.

In real life, it's a Thursday, 11:00 a.m., midsummer, and she has chores.

Store: Eggs, eggplant, dish soap, kitty litter. Money on fridge.
Bathroom: Clean sink, scrub tub.

Love, Mom

The two bills—ten and twenty—fit neatly into her back pocket. She walks along the avenue toward the grocery store. Little plants grow between cracks in the pavement. They move in the breeze as if waving hello. Telephone poles form a roofless colonnade and she strikes every other one with a piece of long grass. After three blocks she comes to a building that was a feed store, then a library. Now it's something else. The cornerstone reads: A.D. 1907. The girl stretches on tiptoes and closes one eye to look in through the grated window. Colored wires spill from rows of shelves, but the wheeled ladders remain; it's a server. Communication embodied. She arrives at the thought all by herself and enjoys the grown-up feeling it gives her. Leaning against the bricks she sucks in her belly and cheeks in order to become an equally resonant image.

Will today be the day? Will she encounter the thing that will change her forever? The limits must be straining at their seams. So many days have passed, one after the other, and all she's done is have some birthdays.

Feeling clots in her throat.

She kicks a small stone into the street and picks up the pace.

All the dogs she sees are leashed.

The car that pulls up behind her is a strange surprise. Its window slides down, revealing an older man in an oxford shirt and wire-rimmed glasses.

"Excuse me, young lady?" His voice is low and friendly. "I was wondering if you could answer a question for me."

Shy and helpful but still androgynous with her fantasy, she steps forward. "Okay, sure."

The man hooks his elbow out the window and leans forward. "I was wondering . . ." he says again. He looks embarrassed; she empathizes.

"What's up?"

"Can I pull down your panties and lick your asshole?"

As the words float from his mouth, the girl's vision vibrates. Her eyes might wobble right out of her head. She places one hand against her own throat for support and the man—now red-faced, sweating—speeds away, toward the on-ramp that leads to the suburbs.

She imagines her mother, at work, selling jewelry and loose diamonds in the mall.

She considers her father, at work, peering at an endless screen and collecting fat around the muscle of his heart.

XIII

Sometimes the girl worries her body is filled with tumors.

Sometimes the girl worries she will grow up and find herself stranded in a woman's body.

Sometimes the girl worries that a bad circumstance will lead to sex with one of her parents.

Sometimes the girl worries she will find a corpse in her closet.

Sometimes the girl worries she will live to see the end of the world.

XIV

She is not ugly, but the coworker's appearance repulses the woman anyway. The bone beneath her gums curves outward and protrudes whenever she smiles. They are both over thirty but the coworker's long, yellow hair gives her the aspect of permanent adolescence.

"I don't smoke either," she says, peeling back the plastic wrap on her microwavable meal. The carton says 200 CALORIES/SERVING in a green font. "In college, someone made an attempt on my life. After that I get afraid whenever I feel like I might not be able to breathe."

Hearing this, the woman slips her fingers along the counter edge in order to pick at its particulate underside. The revelation of this secret has thrown up an impossible divide, and the woman and her coworker are trapped together on its wrong side. Beyond the kitchenette, across the little hall, other nonprofit employees work quietly at their desks.

"I am so sorry that happened to you," she says.

They have just attended a brief presentation for employees on how to maintain their health through middle age.

"I don't really like to talk about it," the coworker says and punches four minutes, forty-four seconds on the microwave. "But you seem like someone who can hear a serious thing and take it in. Come sit with me while I finish this."

"Okay," the woman says. This conversation has filled the woman with panic, but she engages her coworker out of an ageless, perpetual sense of duty.

She arranges her water glass and coffee cup among the objects on her coworker's desk, which include pictures of people who look like her and figurines from television shows the woman recognizes but has never seen. The microwaved food smells very good.

Between bites, the coworker speaks: "Anyways, after I got hired, my therapist said I should find someone at work to tell my story to."

"That makes sense."

"And when I found out you were the client intake person here . . . well, I guess it just sort of clicked for me. Good communicators tend to have more empathy."

"I tell myself that's true," the woman says. Her coworker nods slowly.

"It is. Absolutely." Her eyes are enormous. They look bald, even behind their frosting of mascara. Exhausted, the woman would like to stretch out across the floor and look at her fingers among the carpet fibers. The open floor plan has become overwhelming.

"Thank you," she says.

"Let's go for a walk," the coworker says when her food is gone. "Have you seen the ducks?"

They cross the parking lot, toward the access road, and stop beside a tiny, filthy marsh. It is really just a drainage ditch for runoff from the sprinklers, but it is lined with rushes and sedges. A brown duck with a white pate dips its head under the surface and comes up again, looking oily.

"Three ducks live here. I haven't seen any babies lately, but there were some last year."

The woman looks from the water plants to the culvert pipe, which is slick with algae and a half inch of still water.

"It would be cute if that was their house," she says, lying, and her coworker sighs happily.

"I used to be in a coed fraternity." Her face is now very serious. "I was the only girl but I felt totally like one of the brothers."

Nearby, a maintenance worker starts the trash compactor. The noise drowns out the first half of a crucial sentence but the woman nods, pretending she has heard.

". . . he was on top of me in the hallway, with his hands here." She pantomimes being strangled. "It was so late, and anyway most people had gone home for winter break. The RA walked in just as I was about to pass out and called campus security."

The woman stares at the thick water of the pond. The thought enters her mind that there are some things that should stay private, especially at work.

"Has something like this ever happened to you?"

The woman considers her winter acquaintance from so many years ago. He had been older. Speaking with him, being in his home, had been like pressing herself against the face of a glacier. Had she not gone home and rubbed her humiliation raw against the arm of the couch?

"No," she says, filled with a hatred that billows through her like a cloud of ink. She would like to hurt someone. "But I'm so sorry that happened to you." The duck approaches and rejects a piece of bright plastic among the flotsam in the reeds. Its little eyes do not change shape and then under it goes, headfirst. "Using sex for violence like that . . ."

"He didn't rape me," says the coworker. She frowns. "I thought I said that." The coworker condenses herself into a weird silence. Eventually, she pulls two pieces of gum out of her coat pocket and offers one to the woman, who declines, and puts both pieces into her mouth. Out of the corner of her eye, the woman can see her jaw muscles bunching and relaxing.

"What month is it, again?"

The woman tells her. Clouds mass on the western field of the sky, but the forecast says it will not rain. The woman, too, feels thirsty and dry, and casts herself again into the oily pond. She imagines dragging her toes through the slimy weeds and swallowing a mouthful of floaters and scum.

"It's easy for me to forget these things in the course of my day," says the coworker, then removes the wad from her mouth and flings it into the water.

XV

The woman's back spasms every few feet as she moves down the sidewalk, which makes it difficult to go as fast as she would like.

A pair of teenage girls comes toward her like a bulldozer. Their shapes merge and separate and merge again: jostling, flirting; the one has caught the other in a headlock. The woman is too sore to angle herself quickly out of their way. She braces herself to let them pass, which they do by maneuvering their conjunction left without breaking stride.

The woman eases her body into the gas station. Spots flash at the edge of her vision because she is so hungry. Before this adventure, she had spent nearly the entire day in bed, willing herself to get well and ignoring the painkillers her lover left on their bedside table.

"I've always been bad at being my own parent," she thinks, and self-pity pierces her heart in a way that is almost tasty.

In the candy aisle, she selects a PayDay because it is her father's favorite, and brings it to the counter.

"Just this," she says to the cashier, then goes to eat it on the steps of the blond church near the turn into the cul-de-sac. Chewing thoughtfully, hunched nearly in half, she decides that she will go ahead and call her father.

They have the same body. Besides the back, he has given her his prolific digestive tract and low hairline, though in middle age he developed a bald spot, which his second wife still kisses for luck every morning. The woman has also inherited the downward slant of his upper lip, his short legs and long arms. Even her breasts are his breasts. Her mother—from strapping, Evangelical stock—is flat as a concrete slab.

She dials the number and listens to the ringback. It has been a long time since they've spoken over the phone. As usual, because he takes so long to answer, the woman thinks the connection is bad.

"Dad. Dad. Dad? Dad."

Eventually, he produces his usual response: "Hell-ooo-ooo."

"I'm having your favorite candy bar," she says. "And I did something to my back."

Sugar ticks down the minutes inside her belly and along her gum line. Soon it will come for her brain.

"I saw nine deer in the yard today, plus three babies. I think that's the record so far."

He loves the landscape where she grew up. The woman believes this is because he needs to make up for the circumstances of his Judaism: no one in his family ever worked that land.

Her stepmother has planted strawberries in their backyard, which come later and later every year and are always very small and very sweet.

"That's incredible. What else is going on?"

"Your mother got me to drive her to another doctor's appointment last week," says the woman's father. "Your step-mom didn't like that very much. And I haven't heard from her since. Not even a thank-you."

"That's not very nice," the woman says around her own finger as she picks peanut out of her teeth.

"Do you ever see her husband's boy, anymore? I remember you saying he was strange."

"No," the woman says. Her tone is rough. She has not thought about her erstwhile stepbrother for a long time, and the casual reminder irritates her. "Remember: they got divorced nine years ago. That person and I had nothing in common besides our parents." But, as a spike of blood sugar pushes her into a better humor, she thinks, They are all just other people who live in a big town, surrounded by farmland. "I'm amazed you remember him."

"I remember you talking about him," says her father. "But I only met him the once. He wasn't very personable."

"No," the woman agrees.

"Wouldn't it be nice if we could have dinner tonight?" His slow speech turns her clumsy. She remembers the last time she entered her father's house to celebrate some cozy holiday—Thanksgiving, she decides, because her lover wasn't there and she had slept on the couch—leaking bad faith from every pore.

"It would, but I just ate," the woman says, swallowing more peanut. The kindness and hurt silence on the other end of the line mean that sometime soon he will urge her to come back, to visit, to sleep somewhere within the radius of his love. "Tell me about your back."

"Our back! Funny you should put it that way, but I like it," says her father. If she were a generous, honest person, the woman would correct him. But the words are stuck in her teeth with pieces of caramel and peanut. A janitor emerges from the church and comes straight down the steps to where she's sitting. She picks up the candy wrapper and puts it in her pocket.

"You can't sit here," the janitor says, as though she were a homeless man.

"I'm sorry," she says.

"For what?" says her father.

"I'll just go over there." The woman gestures to the streetlight that has just turned on and casts its green halo against the pink sky and fast-moving clouds. Power lines hum up and down the street; she had not noticed all the water in the air. "Is that far enough?"

"Where are you?" says her father.

"I don't care where you go, as long as it isn't here," says the janitor.

"Fuck off," she mutters as she pulls herself slowly to her feet. She discovers she cannot stand up straight.

"I certainly hope not," says her father and, though it hurts her back, she laughs. All the same, her father wants to know: Is someone hassling her? How long until dark? Has she tried IcyHot?

"It looks like I might be seeing you soon," she says. "I have to help Mom figure out the house."

The woman tries to ignore the sense of capitulation closing around her heart. She knows that her father, like all fathers, craves information beyond the nature of her ailments—the temperature of her breath, for example, or the dimensions of her adult body. The shape of her feet under the yellow blanket, or how long it now takes her to fall asleep, and why.

XVI

Feeling the world a small and comfortless place, the girl leaves the party early. Half drunk, she drives to the lake, which is brownish, shallow, filled with garbage and little fish. Dead pines rustle in the breeze off the water. Orion rises incrementally in the low dome of the sky and indicates to the girl that the winter clock requires a third period with that constellation as its symbol.

A special communication, just for her.

Thinking on this, feeling better, she smokes three cigarettes, throws the butts toward the shoreline, and goes home.

Her stepbrother calls her name as she passes his room. Their parents—his father, her mother—have been asleep for hours.

CFLs blaze in the overhead fixture. He has just bought himself a king-size mattress, and there it is on the floor beneath the windows. The walls are a jagged, electric blue. Pinyon incense burns in the hall bathroom they share, which means he has just taken a dump.

"How are you?" he says. She walks to the window and

looks across the street. The night is unseasonably warm, folded around the family home. There has been rain but no snow. The yard below is waterlogged and sparkling.

"I drove out by the lake. Now I'm here." She wants to tell him about the things she had thought and felt. Haven't they been made family? Neither of them has other siblings.

"I haven't left this room all day," he says.

"What about that?" She gestures with her chin toward the carcass of a rotisserie chicken next to his big computer. He smiles. Through the months her body and his have developed in tandem. No—in conjunction. A new addition on the wall—a rifle mounted next to the closet—makes her feel that she has been gone from home for many years.

"That's been there for a while, now," he says, and the young woman is unsure if he means the gun or the bird.

He and her stepfather have the same downy blond hair. He needs a shave.

"I drove out by the lake," she says again. She needs to speak and here he is. She tells him about the filthy water; she tells him about the constellation and time; she tells him about the red pines. He nods.

"I have something to show you," he says, turns to the monitor, and clicks through a series of prompts.

A video appears in the center of the screen. A middle-aged person with short hair is bent over a hay bale. The young woman is unable to reconcile the bare ass and brown sweater. She tucks her hands into her armpits and finds them damp.

A stallion trots into the picture, flicking its tail. Its erection is huge and piebald and appears jointed in the middle. It rears gently and fits its forelegs over the person's shoulders. The human head bumps rhythmically against a stall partition.

The girl says, "They're fucking."

It is the winter before she starts college and she cannot imagine herself having sex.

The person cries out "Oh! Oh! Oh!" in time with the stallion's thrusts.

The animal finishes and clambers off the small figure whose knees are shaking. Its hooves clatter on the stall floor and the video turns black.

"What do you think of that!" Her stepbrother turns toward her and his eyes look small.

"I think I have to get up early," she says. Her jaw aches.

"Well then, good night!" His clear, bright voice sounds very young, as though he already misses her.

She gets into bed with her clothes on and pulls the covers up to her chin. Furious and wet, she stares at the ceiling, unwilling to even press her legs together as Orion vaults slowly over the rooftops and disappears.

XVII

The woman has devastated her own mouth by not regularly brushing her teeth. This is a holdover from her wild, irrepressible youth.

"See these white stains?" she liked to say, tapping a front tooth with a spoon or the tip of a pencil. "That's from all the fluoride in my hometown's water supply. Thanks to good government, these are like little rocks in my mouth."

But now: consequences. What began as an occasional ache in a molar is now a pain so extreme that it drops her to her knees in the supermarket. She is in the health section, shopping for oral anesthetic in spite of her suspicion that it won't do any good. The spiny shapes in orange and red on a package of energy bars affirm the violence she has done to herself.

Sweating into her T-shirt, the dark threat of rot flickering inside her jaw, the woman feels ashamed. She knows she has been foolish. She thinks, "How did I get to be this age?" Each year no longer bears its own character. Instead, pairs, triplets, quadruplets of years bundle together and accumulate the feeling of different eras during which she has been different people.

Her phone vibrates in her pocket: it is the dentist, calling her back. Focusing on the linoleum, unable to stand or touch the side of her face, she answers.

"I just called in a script for some painkillers," he says. "Take one every six hours and come see me tomorrow."

"I'm already at the pharmacy," she says. "So I guess I'll just wait here until it's ready." Something about her pain necessitates this kind of overexplanation, as though prolonging basic interactions can offer her some kind of relief. She feels blown open.

"Talk to you tomorrow," the dentist says. "Bye now."

The next day the woman crosses a street, a man-made creek, and another street on her way to the dental office. The pills make her itch beneath her eyes and inside her ears and nose and in the spot where her thigh meets her pelvis. She slips into a copse of public sculptures in order to scratch herself without being seen. When she emerges she sees the dental office across the street, a little house with white siding and short hedges.

In the waiting room she fills out a questionnaire and must check YES next to the box that asks if she's ever had a venereal disease.

C-Span flits across the TV screen in the corner.

Within the pink cloud of her pills, the woman considers how much she, too, would like to work there, not because she's interested in teeth but because the office staff are all so friendly, even when they mispronounce her name. It stands to her reason that in order for them to behave so kindly their lives must be both ordered and fulfilling.

She brings the clipboard up to the counter and the receptionist smiles at her. The office lights glaze her perfect teeth and engagement diamond in a blue sheen. Powder makeup dusts the hair on her cheeks.

"You can change the channel any time you like, sweetheart. The clicker's on the shelf," is all she says, but the woman hears a benediction.

She returns to her seat and flips through an article in a homemaking magazine, intermittently scratching her nostrils and armpits. There's a photo of a self-help guru with crispy hair whose teeth are like the dental hygienist's: big and white. A quotation in bold letters has been superimposed on top of it: IT'S NONE OF OUR BUSINESS WHAT THE WORLD DECIDES TO USE US FOR.

The woman prepares to cry, but the office assistant calls her name before her body can produce any tears.

As his fingers slide around inside her mouth, the woman's dentist talks to her about his daughter.

"Boys only want one thing," he says. "I try to tell her that all the time, but you know girls only listen to what you want to hear." His jowls quiver as he leans over her face. She counts his pores, watches his pupils dilate and contract as he adjusts the lamp. "You know her friend got pregnant just last year. Did that boy stick around? No sir, he did not."

The woman can only make a series of sounds in the back of her throat.

"Yeah, indeed," says the dentist, as if he understands. His leg shifts somewhere beneath her head and the drill starts up. Its sound changes when it touches her tooth, but she can't feel anything because of the novocain. The motor stops and a sweet, rotten odor pervades the room: the dying nerve, exposed to the air.

"How old are you? Twenty-three?"

The woman is thirty-three. But the drill drowns out the sound of her guttural grunts.

"Don't worry," the dentist says. "You're the only one who can smell it."

XVIII

At the far end of the counter, a cluster of white narcissus erupts in a ceramic pot. Their musk and brightness thrust the café's interior into a different season. Outside, too late in the year, it is finally snowing.

Because she doesn't know how to drink coffee, the girl orders tea.

"You look taller," the man says when he takes her money. He is clean-shaven tonight, but his long, rough hair reminds her of a witch. He deposits change into the girl's palm without touching her. Can he read the feeling in any of her gestures? Maybe her lust and embarrassment smell like all the clefts of her body at once.

She carries her drink to a table near the door and sits down. She knows little about him besides what she has observed from afar. Other customers—women and girls and several young boys—also want him, but manage to make their desire useful. They bring him little gifts: cigarettes, candy, brown bags of liquor, and, of course, extra tips. The girl is old enough to see that he encourages their affection but too young to understand why.

The man goes out the front door with a snow shovel. It is difficult for the girl to look at his entire body when it moves. Instead, she watches the snow and thinks of the dark countryside, of the plains with their diminished farms and abandoned outbuildings.

The girl swallows the rest of her tea and stands to leave. She has not even pretended to read her book. The man intercepts her at the threshold.

"Why are you leaving me already?" he says. He has never spoken to her in this way. Snowflakes rime his eyelashes. The girl knows that between them, he is the prettier.

"I'm done with my drink."

"So go and come back. I'll be closed by midnight."

"Okay," the girl says.

At home her mother has been asleep for several hours. The house is dark and quiet. The girl goes to the toilet and shits herself empty, then sits in the living room with all the lights off until is it time to go back, where he waits beneath a floodlight, his coat open at the neck, as though his long body belongs in the cold.

"This is my mom's car," the girl says as he climbs in.

"Isn't that nice."

Inside his apartment everything is shabby and spare. She follows him down a tiny hallway, through a doorway with hinges but no door. The place smells strongly of a human body and of old oil and incense, and the girl thinks she was right: he is like a witch.

In the bedroom he takes off his boots and coat and sits on the edge of the bed, a futon on a homemade platform. In place of a headboard, he has tacked a garland of dried flowers on the wall.

"Sit with me," he says and, in a movement that betrays his strength, which in turn betrays his masculinity, bundles her tightly onto his lap. The girl cannot locate her intelligence.

"What . . . what did you do in school?" she says. An outdated map of Europe and Asia hangs on the opposite wall.

"I studied mushrooms," he says into her ear. A laugh percolates in the back of the girl's throat and she gags. Mushrooms! His hair is so pungent she can hardly breathe. He has one hand on her waist and another on her thigh. She can feel his heartbeat against her back, his erection under the seat of her jeans.

Fear swells her desire until it forms a monstrous shape inside her. He has told her before: he is nearly thirty. She has never touched anyone's breasts but her own, has never seen a penis in real life.

"I call them skin-needles, because they poke you and prick you and fill you with goo," said a classmate who hadn't seen her father for seven years.

As she remembers this, the girl's vagina opens and closes like a fist. It feels warm and alive, the opposite of a hole.

"I have to pee," she says.

"Hurry back." Frozen by sarcasm, his tone indicates this will be her only chance. He releases her body from his grasp. Receptive and dominant, eyes closed, he lays himself back among the pillows. She imagines the secret fruit of his body—his penis like a big weeping thumb behind his fly.

The bathroom is so cold that ice glazes the windowpanes above the tub. Stretch marks inside her thighs have turned purple. Between her knees, her underwear is slick and odorless. She tries to urinate but produces only a thin stream. Her neck hurts with the awareness that she has done nothing to deserve this opportunity and will do nothing to bring it to fruition. She knows that she will be home soon in the dark house with its sleeping mother, hysterically intact.

XIX

After an acceptable insertion that led, eventually, to mutual but isolated orgasms, the woman's lover has gone to run his weekend errands, and she has entered the bathroom to perform the ablution of flushing her urethra with urine and cleaning residue off her patch.

As she goes, she thinks about the consistency with which the lover gets food stuck in his front teeth, his sensitivity, and his unflappable kindness. After sex, she often thinks about love, about being peeled back, exposed to someone else's deepest feelings and having no respite from being wanted.

The problem, she thinks, is that it's impossible to remember the lover's dark interior is not hers.

The woman moves through the house to do the weekend's picking up. She is holding some mismatched pair of socks in one hand and a stack of junk mail in the other. If she isn't careful, she'll put all of it in the recycling bin because she is ruminating.

How had fucking worked between them, those years ago? Suddenly generous in her desire for desire, the woman tries to conjure up the original shape of their lust without all of love's neutering reliability. She looks at the objects in her hands that now include a dark, hairy sweater and a popular paperback novel, and drops them on the coffee table. She opens the windows to feel the breeze while she scratches her face and head.

This is the story as she remembers it:

They had met at a friendly potluck. She'd brought bread and butter, which she had decided was a laudably unexpected but essential choice. When she'd entered the dining room, he had turned up his face from the table where he was sitting with friends of friends of friends. A tiny, dense pendulum swung between them. It was like being struck both between the eyes and right in the pussy. She looked at his dark brows and the white column of his throat. There was something in him of a friendly animal, and of architecture, and of the feeling of a telephone vibrating optimistically in her pocket. There was something in him of herself as a port for the force of her desire, which had always been sudden and, the woman thinks, until lately, irrevocable.

Behind her left ear the woman heard the sound of her mother's voice saying her name in the morning.

And, as though God were very much alive and benevolent and horny, the person sitting next to him had gotten up to see about a dish in the oven. The man who was not yet her lover moved his plate to make room, and the woman sat down into a puddle of feeling that slid vertically down from the crown of her head all the way through the arches of her feet.

If the woman and her lover are together socially when she

tells this story, she will reach sweetly to touch him at this point, to perform the myth of their origin for an audience. "I was suddenly very aware—his leg is next to my leg! I had never spent so much time noticing a knee," she will say and smile like she can hardly believe her good fortune.

They had gone joyfully to fuck in the first minutes of their first date. She sat first on his lap, nearly ruining the crotch of her white pants, and then on his face. They fucked until she was puffy and sore. In the weeks following, her lust made a red volcano at the back of her head. She became drowsy with the need for sex; she couldn't sleep.

There have, of course, been other people, and the woman remembers them kindly, but nothing had been like this. She had been young enough to think that love would always be a rack of pleasure and anticipation and so she had spread her legs and opened her mouth and swallowed a whole bellyful of it.

He is the only man who has ever ejaculated inside her. It happened first as a dirty revelation, the feeling of wetness swimming inside wetness, pleasure like a sugar cube dissolving in the mouth.

But even this most intimate, repulsive trespass has finally lost its luster. Their love has come to rest somewhere on a spectrum between a cell phone contract and a collaboration.

If the woman could see, like a person with good eyes and a capacity for attention, she would see that the scene in her favorite windowpane is made entirely of plants. She would recall from her horticulture magazine that plants are always in the process of fucking because how else could a limited creature—rooted to its spot—possibly respond?

XX

A man with a black wool jacket, a powerful position, and a terminal illness.

A man with a habit of smoking cigarettes on the toilet after sex.

A man with excellent technique and a baby in a different country.

A man with long, shapely hands and a compulsion toward hard work.

A woman with high little breasts, two muscular dogs, and no pubic hair.

A boy with a shaved head and a penis like a bar of gold inside his pants.

A girl with an all-white apartment and a bumpy tongue.

A boy with blackheads on his back and a job in the bookstore.

XXI

Looking at her lover, the woman would like to know: Are you a wolf or a well? Are you a labyrinth or a series of nesting dolls, masquerading as a man?

He doesn't answer because she hasn't asked.

They are lying end to end on the white couch in the family room watching dusk settle around the neighborhood. Someone their age escorts a toddler up and down the sidewalk. The child has a tuft of grass clenched in one hand. An indecipherable sound comes out of its head. Upon hearing the sound, the woman does not feel any corresponding tug inside her uterus. How could she? Her lover's profile is framed here against the decorative hearth, not there in the TV screen of the window. Gestating their relationship is more than enough to keep her occupied.

Cloud pink, poison thundering inside their seeds and blossoms, the trumpet flowers have bloomed beneath the open windows. When he comments on their odor, the woman reminds her lover their pollen gives sleeping people bad dreams.

"So I've heard," he says, and wiggles her baby toe between

his thumb and forefinger. She often tells him the same thing over and over, to inoculate him with her worldview. "I should just tear this freaky little thing off," he says and, drowsy with contentment, she yawns. The living room is so good; the woman, lately, is feeling so good. She likes this optimistic house they live in. She likes especially its midcentury nooks and crannies, like the little alcove in the hallway that holds mystery and candles and the crawl space under the porch "for hiding bodies and every one of our secrets," as her lover says, pantomiming every time, somehow, a slit throat and every ounce of his sentimentality.

The woman is proud that, together, they have filled the place with objects that tell a story of their combined sensitivity and taste.

The lover turns on the brass standing lamp. It flares over them like a dinky sun and hurts the woman's eyes. The neighbor and the child are gone—or maybe they are just obscured by the bright reflection in the newly black window.

In a different neighborhood, sirens articulate the truth, that this rental house is only a temporary refuge. The woman converts their domestic future into a reservoir of nostalgia, to be drawn from when she needs to protect her finer feelings.

A happy projection materializes.

Soon the lover will rise from the couch to prepare their supper of frozen cod, salad, and some kind of golden pilaf. The food will taste good because he always cooks with real butter, real sugar, and plenty of salt. He will consume no more than his fill, and as she watches him eat, the woman will understand that his thinness comes from satisfaction.

It will be after 10:00 p.m. by the time they're through with the dishes, and she will shower while he brushes his teeth. She will open the window above the bathtub and look out onto the shingles of the carport and the non-native tree-tops clustered around it.

On the other side of the shower curtain, the lover will spit toothpaste into the toilet instead of the sink, plant a foot on the tub, and urinate on top of the froth in the bowl. After her shower, the woman will trim her pubic hair and pluck her bristliest whiskers into the lurid cocktail, replace the lid, and flush everything down.

This ritual will be more intimate and less disquieting than sex.

She will emerge shorn and rosy and naked from the hall into the white rectangle of their bedroom. He will already be in bed, the dog curled against his side, and his feet will make a little mountain under the sheets. Before sleep, he will play with her shortened bush as though it were a lock of his own hair.

Overnight, the little old house will settle around them. It needs a new foundation, but that will never be their problem.

In the morning, the lover will wake up furious. The woman will go make coffee and flip backward through a horticulture magazine addressed to a previous tenant. She will accumulate more factoids to offer him on her platter of affection when he finally comes downstairs. In return, he will unfurl himself before her a little more every day. She supposes this means someday she will know him completely. Or maybe, they will both just die.

XXII

Maybe the chef had excused himself from the line, gone to the bathroom, pushed a hemorrhoid back inside his body, and had forgotten to wash his hands.

The tuna steak had been delicious and expensive, ruby colored, dusted with pistachios.

"Bucket," the woman says.

After hours of the same thing, her lover executes the routine perfectly. He makes it to her side of the bed just as she slumps out from under the covers, head first, toward the floor. She vomits yellow bile into the blue bucket.

"Good girl," he says soothingly. "There you go. Good girl. Maybe now you can eat something."

He uses the same tone to coax her toward orgasm.

When she's done she rests her sweaty face against his knee and watches a thread of saliva soak into his jeans. His hands are cool and dry, stroking her back, lifting up one heavy breast and then another. It feels good because her back aches from throwing up; it feels bad because illness has returned the woman to childhood. She cannot think of herself as any kind of receptacle.

Her lover tucks her back into bed and goes to get the pretzels. Beneath the duvet, the top sheet lies in a greasy rope around her feet. Nausea roosts in the hinge of the woman's jaw and at the base of her skull, and she knows its color is yellow, a gaseous yellow, a spongy yellow, a fibrous yellow, a hairy yellow . . .

The world, made very narrow by and reflected in the eye of her sickness:

The little bedroom is decked with plants and books and artwork made by talented peers whom she now despises for their health and contentment. The dresser is there, too, tucked under the picture window, an object infested with other objects in the crowded room. The thought blooms inside her mind, filling up her sinuses, clogging the space behind her soft palate. Her father seems to stand in the doorway, watching her. Without her glasses she cannot see his face or identify his clothing. He holds a basket and steps forward to offer up its contents—two small, naked animals. By their shaky movements, the woman can tell the creatures are blind.

"Mole rats," she says and feels them on her breasts, trying to warm themselves in the heat from her fever. All her joints feel made of glass.

"You're my little mole rat," her lover says, striding across the room, carrying a full glass and a shallow bowl. "Are you feeling like a snack?"

He has fed himself throughout the day in this room—first

oatmeal, then soup and a sandwich——and is now eating one of her pretzels and lubricating the mouthful with golden beer. He stands beside the bed, swallows, and belches quietly. The odors of masculinity and yeast enter her nose and the woman can't help it, she thinks again of her father. She imagines him topped with a yellow hat and emits a precarious fart.

"Toilet," she says.

Her lover helps her down the hall and into the bathroom. Matter flows out of her and into the bowl. It is loose and uncomfortable and the source feels endless. It unspools inside her and she must also throw up, this time into the small trash can her lover has placed devotionally at her feet.

Eventually she feels herself empty and rests her cheek against the wall. She looks at the marble-pattered tile on the floor until a splotch of pigment turns into a cartoon rat. It seems to be giving her a thumbs-up, and makes her feel a little better. The bright smells of bleach and toilet cleaner slice into her stupor. It feels good to be alone with her body in this dim, cool room. But she can hear her lover on the other side of the door, the floorboards creaking beneath his weight.

XXIII

On days like today, the woman imagines bathing in a vat of seltzer, bubbles to stimulate her raw scalp, scrub the oily residue away from her inner ears, and soothe the sore places on her cheeks and head where she has scratched and scratched and scratched as the itch recedes deeper, or shifts to the right, or prickles to the left, subcutaneous and autoimmune.

She is sitting on the couch in her living room, alone in the house. She has taken the day off to sit with her misery. Her lover is at work, concocting yet another website, and her eyes are streaming. There is a crust in her ear and a scab on her scalp where she has scratched herself. Her nose is red, her eyes are red.

If she leaves the house, well-meaning strangers might ask if she is unwell or has been crying.

In the alcove and on the coffee table, candle wax is collecting dust. A lancet of sunlight comes in through the top of the blinds in the living room window, into the dark family room where the dog has gotten footprints on the white couch, where the crown molding and quarter round betray their fineness by gathering more dust and hair.

The woman has left a trail of wet tissues throughout the house. Her ear hurts and she is afraid of getting grime in the scab. In the bedroom she had blown her nose in clothes from the hamper. Wadded up in the hall: three soaking wet T-shirts, three old socks, two bandanas.

This is the burden of being a body.

Desperate, she goes to sit at the kitchen table because it is made of metal and glass and a little bit of plastic and rests her hot, leaky face against it. To soothe herself, she picks at the familiar scab on the crown of her head. It has been with her now for a week. She will not let it heal because picking it provides a meditation, a needle of pain, and sometimes it seems she might pass through its eye and into some better dimension.

The kitchen is at one end of a short hallway that terminates in the front door. Through the double panes she can see the blue back of the mail carrier (just leaving) and the white truck parked across the street. She must bring the mail inside or some stranger might steal it.

The cuffs of her soft pants wrap themselves around her feet as the woman shuffles to the door. When she unlocks it, the sound of the bolt sliding back is metallic and good.

Sunlight burns the raw spots on the woman's eyelids and the chafe below her nostrils. At this time of day, the contrast is extreme and casts things into their simplest antagonisms: light and dark, hard and soft, mineral and animal.

Her vision finds its relief in landing upon objects that are not biological: the black shingles and shiny windows of every house; the rubber tires of every car; the dryness of the pavement.

The woman should have been an object. Her brain is bad, her mind is stupid, her speech is cumbersome.

Meanwhile, the neighborhood continues its broad, beautiful spread. Every piece of verdure is in some stage of blossom or decay. The woman thinks of spores and of pollen in helixes, soft-looking ovoids, little puffs—all pastel, in her imagination—in this climate where nothing goes dormant, but plants and animals die and their bodies are carpeted with mold and dark fungus.

The woman sneezes, wipes her nose and mouth with the back of her hand, and sneezes again. She thinks about someone she knows—she cannot remember who—describing an orgasm as a sneeze of the crotch, and uses it as further proof that there is no one who understands her predicament.

She has love, there are people in her life, but their input is never helpful.

"I don't have allergies," said the strong friend, his well-muscled arms relaxing beneath their homegrown red pelt.

"I've heard exercise can have an impact on these things," said her mother. "I remember that was always part of your problem."

"What about taking some Claritin?" said her pretty-necked friend with the perfect taste.

"There are shots you can get. If you have insurance. Do you

have insurance?" said the oldest friend, texting from far away. "Or make a tincture. Or smoke a cigarette and you won't even notice anymore that you have to sneeze."

"We really should get you an air purifier or something," said the lover, brimming as usual with something called "a solution."

Give it a rest! thinks the woman, because she is so tired.

But she needs to put her body to its purpose. She needs to acclimate. She has been here in town for long enough, it should be any day, any week, any month, any year now.

XXIV

The woman meant to tell her pretty-necked friend about her upcoming trip and all her misgivings, but the conversation turns to celebrities.

"I don't know what you like so much about him," says the friend, receiving her glass of white. A ring is flashing. As usual, her neck is incredible. "Especially now he's not even that handsome. He's been famous for decades and he's a terrible actor. Plus his nose reminds me of a tulip."

"He's always been my favorite one," the woman says softly. Sipping her drink and then her soup, tasting their bad combination, she continues. "I read an article about him last week that called him the last movie star."

It is better to talk about him and not about her mother. He reminds her of being very young, when life unfurled before her as a vast prairie, rustling with secrets. The woman remembers seeing him for the first time. From a small position on the floor, looking up. She had been stroking her babysitter's shaved legs and looking at the movie poster on the girl's wall. Too young for any definite sexual feeling, the

woman had believed that the long, golden cowboy in the photograph would like her very much. That he would take her
onto his lap and into his confidence.

She hardly ever thinks about what the actor might be like
in real life, and does not like to consider his equally famous
ex-wife or their bevy of multinational children. He is so beautiful, so excellently dressed, that the woman cannot imagine
pleasing herself using his body. As though her desire would
contaminate an otherwise pure experience.

"Good," says her friend.

At home alone, still full from lunch, the woman slices a
sour green apple into a bowl and eats it while she watches the
trailer for the actor's new movie on her laptop.

He plays a drifter who floats down a highway in a big,
dumpy car. The character occupies a series of dark motel
rooms with high little windows and low lamps, first a red
room, then a white room, then a blue room, and, finally, a
black room.

"Things went funny for me a while back," he says in voice-
over, then moves into the shot. His long, dirty hair catches
light from the mammoth sky.

This character—a murderer and equal opportunity
rapist—lacks charisma. The woman inspects the preview for
the actor's usual sparkle, his optimism, and cannot find it.
Each close-up indicates that he once had bad skin.

His body shocks her. He has a ponderous belly and little
tits budding beneath his filthy T-shirt. The woman thinks he
must have taken this role so he could, finally, allow himself
to change.

Framed as a bust in the preview's final shot, the character finishes a cheeseburger after pulverizing a teenager's neck and chest with a cinder block.

The woman's lover has said, many times: "He's so good at eating on camera. I would watch a whole movie with him in it, just eating. It's like he's never had to think about what he looks like to other people."

This is still true, though the preview conveys a sense of animalism and not the effortlessness of beautiful people. The woman feels like laughing when the actor licks his fingers clean. Drying his hands in his hair, he shuffles through a parking lot toward the implacable plains, and the trailer ends.

The movie will be released in July, pitted against the season's biggest blockbusters.

After she watches twice more, she closes the browser window, revealing her desktop: a photograph of her lover smiling as though the woman were behind the camera, which she was not. Feeling like her insides are sunburned, the woman closes her laptop, puts her bowl in the sink, and goes into her living room. She takes off her clothes to look at her body in the mirror. Her big breasts point at the floor.

The formative flirtations of childhood will never happen again.

There are jobs she will never know how to do.

The last movie star has grown old and fat.

Elsewhere in the house, the woman's phone vibrates into an empty room. Her friend has messaged to say, "I'm sorry if I offended you. Maybe next time you can tell me about your mom."

The woman knows that at some point she will go see the movie. She will go alone. It will not be masturbatory because it will not be pleasurable. It will be like being in church or temple or an AA meeting—sitting in an audience, awaiting further communication.

XXV

The housing development is on top of a hillock and, if it were daytime, the woman would convince herself she could see the curvature of the earth. In this part of the country, distance zeroes in like a countdown until perspective goes bad. But in the dark she feels close to the face of outer space, and the evening chill is an excellent balm for the new pimples glistening upon her chin.

The woman shifts from one foot to another because her thighs and back are aching, maybe from all the sitting and driving, though there is also the telltale heaviness beneath her belly button she's carried around all day; a female lump of shot, poised for its moment.

The woman would like to ride a thick shaft—a polished wood baton or an unmelting icicle—until the shot dissolves. Her vulva and asshole are itchy. Her breasts are heavier, even, than usual. She radiates indecency, exists outside any normal parameters, though tonight she must make conversation. She could chew and swallow a whole lemon.

Her father's house is glowing in the nighttime, and the

woman can see into the kitchen. Her stepmother is stand-ing at the sink with her head tilted to one side. The door is locked, though the woman knows there's a key under the mat. These people are unafraid without being fearless, and when she is both well-fed and rested she understands their position.

Enough of a guest to have brought a bottle of wine, the woman rings the bell, and the door opens so quickly she feels embarrassed.

"You're here! She's here!" Her father's wife sounds sur-prised by her own excitement. She is smiling; she is medium-sized and attractive; she looks nothing like the woman's mother; and each of her gestures contains a request for a hug. "Gosh you and your dad look more and more alike every time I see you."

She refers to the shape of their hands, their spindly necks and solid Jewish arms, the round faces and round noses. No, there is no question of the patrilineage that has ordered the woman's blood.

In the kitchen, the woman's father mills around inside his pleasure at seeing her, smiling the whole time and nearly silent. He fusses with the foil seal on the wine; he unfolds and refolds a towel on the countertop; he puts some dishes away but stops before the rack is empty.

It feels like a violation to watch her father struggle inside his evening's happiness, and the woman regards his aging face until his image detaches from his concept and he seems like a stranger. As a child, she often found it useful to do this trick with people and also with familiar words, saying them over and over until they lost meaning, usually words like "thank you" or "dog" or "me."

When they finally embrace, the firmness of her father's hug hurts the woman's tender breasts. For help, she looks over his shoulder at the shaded Y above the television, where the seams of wall and ceiling come together. Beyond that little apex, stars cartwheel through the cold sky.

"Let's sit in the family room," he says into her ear. He leads her there by steering her left shoulder, saying there are things—"old objects" are the words the woman hears but not the ones he uses—to take home with her. The woman's step-mother politely mutes the TV. "I thought that now you had come back you might want these," says her father. It has been nearly a year and a half since they've seen each other.

On the table are two items: a pocketknife and a tattered book that had pulled the woman through adolescence. He picks up the knife—a red Victorinox—and unfolds the old blade. "You'll have to check your bag or mail this to yourself at the gate. Be careful with it; it's easy to get too comfy when a blade is this dull." He closes the knife and hands it to her.

"I remember this," she says, because she does, and as she slips it into her own pocket she recrosses her right leg over her left to give her gut a break from the waistband of her pants.

"Your mother gave me that," he says, and the woman knows that will be the only time he mentions her. He will not ask the woman about her mother in front of his wife, which is strange because their marriage is unassailable. It strikes the woman as funny, as so perfect, this human foible—the stupid ways people respect each other. "And that damn book. I think when you were twelve it was the only thing you read all year." That he has carried this memory for so long is just proof of his endless patience. This feeling of being had into a house, of benefitting from her father's kindness and long memory, reminds the woman of being on a good drug. She could almost relax. She could almost touch his hand and tell him how good it is to see him.

But the shot swells inside her pelvic basket and scrambles her insides. Her jeans are as tight as they've ever been. Gas congeals into a storm system waiting for its moment to emerge.

"Should we open the wine?"

"Let me get the glasses." The woman is eager to display her helpfulness in this house where she has never lived and also to escape the living room so she can fart in peace. She stands and the timer finally goes off, the seal finally ruptures: a hot rush tumbles down and out to soak the crotch of her pants.

In the antiseptic refuge of the guest bathroom, the blood is so fresh it doesn't smell. Of course there are no tampons: the woman's stepmother hasn't menstruated in years. And the woman is incapable of planning ahead, never keeps anything on hand that might benefit herself in the future or that might satisfy the constant, childish demands of her body. She winds toilet paper around her palm and fits it between her labial cleft and her ruined underwear.

The woman returns to her father and his wife and stands with her blood-bright ass to the door.

"I'm so sorry," she says. "But I have to go out."

Her father looks at his wife, who is already touching his arm to stem the waves of his disappointment.

"Dinner will be ready in about fifteen minutes." The woman's father can only speak to his wife, the translator. "Isn't that what you said?" He looks as sad as a deflated balloon.

"I'll come back as fast as I can."

"Honey you go and come back. We'll put a plate in the oven," she says. Now it is a conversation between them as women, which the woman abhors. The father is back inside the silent tent of his masculinity, though it was his sperm that made the woman a woman in the style of all the women in his family. She remembers learning that his mother, too, had had difficult periods.

"I'm bleeding," she says to him. Somehow she is communicating, not beseeching. Her voice tolls like a bell in the room. "And I don't have anything, and you don't either."

The woman watches her father rise from out of the sad story he tells himself about his love for her. The woman knows that if she peered closely enough, she would see a tiny version of her face, which is his face, reflected precisely in the pupil of each of his eyes. She is a human woman who came from his body and his desire. Her nose burns. She could cry but instead just emits more blood into her jeans.

"You go and come back," says the father to the woman, his child.

XXVI

The woman needs her plug and, as it always does, the tamed countryside provides. Tonight providence looks like a gas station glowing under the moon.

A huge, dark cube squats at the far end of the parking lot, abutted by fields made pale by the night. For a moment the woman assumes it is a shipping container, but she realizes that she can see through it to the halogen lamps on its other side—and no shipping container would be ringed by a high fence wrapped with barbed wire.

The cube, she realizes, is a cage.

Its presence absorbs logic. The woman can feel it happening behind her as she walks, thick with blood and apprehension, toward the storefront, where half a sign in the window reads: THEY HAVE BEEN PART OF OUR FAMILY FOR OVER 15 YEARS.

Inside, to the right of the door, is an easel with a corkboard covered with photos of a lion in the various stages of his life—as a cub; asleep on the belly of a man in a lawn chair; sprawled in a driveway as a bulky adolescent; as an adult in the cage, yawning behind the bars while a little girl mimics his expression.

A stuffed female in a glass box on a homemade shelf presides over the peanuts. Merchandise—travel mugs, baseball hats, sunglasses—emblazoned with a five-toed paw print—hangs from a rack attached to the bottom of the shelf, and by the time the woman approaches the counter with her box of floral tampons her curiosity has outgrown her skepticism.

"Do you really have a lion?"

The attendant is younger than the woman. Because it is her work, she cannot experience this enchantment, the promise of a lion where there should be no lion.

"I mean, he's not mine. But there is one here, if you want to see him."

For guidance, the woman turns to the picture board one more time. She goes into the bathroom for insertion and and clean-up—stuffs her stiff underwear into the pocket of her coat and emerges back among the shelves. She pretends to inspect a pack of gum, then wanders bashfully back to the counter, where the attendant stands unfooled by the performance.

"I think I'd like to see him," she says, and hands over more money. She should be in a hurry to get back to dinner, but she is not. Her father has waited for months; another thirty minutes won't make any difference.

The cashier retrieves a Styrofoam container from a mini-fridge behind the counter and a plastic spoon from the coffee station, and presents both to the woman.

"What's in this?"

"Hamburger and antibiotics."

They walk together out of the store and across the parking lot toward the spectacle. Ears ringing, the woman prepares for a communion with the predatory nature of the universe. Or a distant relative. And she is a little afraid. She considers the rotten underwear in her pocket. What if it inspires a combination of arousal and bloodthirst in this lion, this robust solar male, and that's how she goes out? She imagines the scene: mauled to death, blood seeping from her open throat and parted legs—and smiles idiotically.

At first there is nothing to see. The attendant stands near the gate with one leg crossed behind the other and rests her head against the fence post.

"There's a tray right in front of you," she says. "You can take as many pictures as you want but don't put your hand inside the bars and don't use a flash."

The spoon is too flimsy to maneuver through the cold meat so the woman uses her fingers. Meat gets under her nails. Would the lion prefer a mound or a patty? She plops a rough dollop into the tray and imprints it with her menstrual fingertips.

She shoves the tray through its slot and settles back onto the cold asphalt to wait, hands clasped around her knees.

A security light on a motion sensor jumps on to reveal movement inside the cage.

As the lion hauls itself upright and into the light, its belly swings back and forth, inches from the ground. Rough patches show through the fur on its elbows. Tiny, useless testicles cluster at the base of its tail. They are dwarfed by the vastness of its size because the lion is obese.

The woman knows she has done something wrong, and there is no one she can ask for forgiveness. The lion will eat what she has fed it, and then eat some more. She wants to absolve herself by crying, but the attendant is still nearby, a silhouette breaking off the tips of her hair.

"What an old man," says the woman.

"He's five," says the silhouette.

The animal will not look at either of them and will not approach the food. Instead, he heaves himself the length of the cage and back, swinging his massive head. A rear foot turns in the same place each time. The woman wonders how many more years it will take until he wears a divot in the concrete.

"Have you had him . . . the whole time?"

"He was born here, if that's what you mean. They had another one before that." Speaking of this gas station history, the girl sounds a hundred years old.

The lion lifts the bony strand of his tail and sprays a section of the fence. A breeze whips up the smell of hot ammonia and concrete and evening clover from the surrounding fields, and the lion grimaces to better take in the scent, licking the inside of his mouth. His teeth look pink in the jagged light.

The woman does not cover her nose because her hands, too, are fragrant with meat and old blood.

She feels herself growing older.

Through the bars of the cage, through the links in the fence, a grain silo pushes darkly through the air like an alien monument. In the distance, towns present themselves only as lights twinkling in the darkness. The moon has fallen some millimeters and should be screeching but it is silent.

XXVII

The mother is in a meeting with many other people around a long table, and the child is very bored. Despite her mother's assertions, she knows that an hour is a long time.

"When can we go home?" says the child, lips close to her mother's fragrant temple.

"I can barely stand your negativity this morning," says her mother, and directs her to go somewhere—anywhere— else. "If you would, please," she says, and the child knows it's important.

Outside, the land radiates the feeling of crops growing and also the sounds of wind and insects. None of the tourists have arrived because it isn't quite summer. All the two-story buildings along the main street are still asleep.

The child is relieved of her loneliness when she sees the big familiar person smoking on the bench.

"What's up, Little Bit," says the person, whom the child likes very much. She offers the child the slab of her palm in a low five.

"I'm supposed to wait out here," says the child, noting in

her own mind that this isn't quite true. "Until the meeting is over."

The big person's expression doesn't change, but she says, "Well, I got my little mister in the car if you care to take a look."

The big person is like an excellent pirate. She has two gold teeth on top and a keloid necklace because someone once stabbed her in the throat and left her for dead in a big field. The girl knows this because she's been to many meetings, and, when there aren't any suitable adults around, her mother tells her the best gossip.

"Can we take him for a walk?" The child looks at the primer stains on the person's canvas pants. The words "Would you please be my babysitter?" are dangerously close to dropping from her mouth.

"Can't, Bitsy. Gonna finish this smoke and head inside; I'm already late. But I'll see you after." She crushes her smoke beneath one of her big boots and hoists herself off the bench. The girl knows the woman's back hurts because she works so hard—she's even got a velcro brace under her big T-shirt. Watching her recede up the sidewalk and into the church, the girl decides that today she will ask her mother for a very short haircut and a pair of boots.

The big person has parked her old Jeep right near the entrance, and the child concludes that it isn't far enough away to get her in trouble.

"Hi, little mister," she says to the hairy mutt on the front seat. She taps the window softly, makes the kissing sound with her lips. When he covers his tiny nuts with his tail, the girl knows that something in their transaction has gone wrong. Again, the girl taps on the glass and his shivering intensifies. He won't even bark. The dog's eyes bulge, and the child rummages around inside her heart for some affection but cannot find it.

The girl grinds her teeth. If she were here, the girl's mother would roll her eyes and call it useless. The girl cannot believe the big, excellent person would have a dog like this dog. She feels betrayed but also sickened, a little sorry for the big person.

A hot column of anger tickles the girl from her vagina to the back of her throat. If the little dog were outside the car she would chase it into the street. Everyone is still inside the meeting, crying or laughing or staring at the ceiling fans.

The child turns back to the window, in which her own reflection overlaps the image of the dog on the seat.

"Little mister," she says again, tapping to keep his attention. "Little mister." If she could, she'd stuff his whole head into her mouth and bite down. She wants to use all the curse words she knows but all she can do is clear her throat.

"Try to pull yourself together. If you would, please," the child says. The words come out tinny and flat. She knows she should have the voice of man or the howl of a predator, but she is just a shabby little girl and this is the only tone she can muster. To make up for it she taps harder and stares into the dog's bulging eyes, willing her rage through the glass and into his walnut brain. He cannot look away from her. His ears are flat, tail tucked hard between his tiny haunches. He trembles so violently that he cannot even walk across the seats to escape.

The girl expects that the mutt will look away but instead he just pisses all over the seat.

XXVIII

Through the woman's new haze of resentment (she is tired, the flight home was long), all the angles of the dog's elegant, dished face seem like a mean trick. The woman reaches across her own legs to push the gummy lips into a grimace.

Motionless at the end of the bed, the dog just stares into the dark hall. Her lip has stuck hilariously to a cuspid, but the woman can't laugh because she believes the dog has come to prefer her lover.

"What a savage," she says. "These days I'm sort of beside the point, right?"

When he finally comes back from his shower, balls bouncing, using the towel to dry his hair, the dog shows him her fawn-colored belly and funny smile.

"What a manipulator," the woman says. "What a little slut." Her voice has pitched to an insane octave. It is a bright color alongside the bright white walls of the bedroom, which usually seem so chic to her, practically Mediterranean, but now seem bald and bland and bad.

Holding the towel over his crotch, the lover clucks and

bends to blow air into the dog's face. "That's the whole point," he says. "It's so we don't eat you. Isn't that right?"

The dog answers him by rubbing her muzzle with both front paws and wagging so hard dust spurts from the duvet cover when her tail thumps it.

The woman wraps her arms around the dog's body and drags her across the mattress, over a hump of bedding, and into her lap. The woman takes the tip of an ear between her teeth and bites down until the dog squirms.

"She had gigantic nipples when I got her, did I ever tell you that?" The woman buries her face in the dog's scruff, lavishes her muzzle and egg-smelling ears with kisses. "Like Mike and Ikes, but pink." She resurfaces and scrapes the hair off her lips. Propped on an elbow, she stage whispers: "Why don't you ever tell us what happened to your babies?"

This gruesome performance is not playacting. Trapped behind her own forehead, wavering between an encapsulated past and a distorted future, the woman does not feel like a warm-blooded animal. She had gotten the dog to ease her loneliness, and it had worked for a long time, filling her life with cockleburs and grit in the sheets, the organic smell of warm fur, the pure pleasure of watching the dog root among bushes or wiggle across a lawn, sneezing with excitement.

But not anymore.

The woman's lover does not offer his own rejoinder, which means that he does not wish to partake in her fantasy. Instead, he goes to their dresser and puts on a pair of underpants. The woman thinks he must not want her seeing his nakedness.

"I think you look good today," she says.

"Do you still want to take her to the park?"

"No," the woman says, because she would like the dog to learn a little gratitude. "Just let her do it in the yard." She disengages herself from the bedclothes.

Dog hair covers her black sweat suit and puffs into the air as she goes downstairs to the pantry, where she has hidden a bag of stinky, expensive treats behind a box of old pasta. Her lover does not know they exist and she will never tell him.

The bag crinkles as she opens it and the dog rushes into the kitchen, her whole body bristling with anticipatory pleasure. She dances in one place, nails rapping the floor. The woman leads her toward the table and sits down with a fist under her chin. She looks down at the dog as she remembers being looked at by adults—with a magisterial displeasure just short of cruelty. One at a time, she feeds the dog smaller and smaller morsels until the animal is licking only taste from her fingers.

XXIX

One day, the woman passed by the empty lot and saw one stray dog humping another, surrounded by flowers. And she thought: "I also want a transformative friendship."

One day, the woman entered her own kitchen and saw a mouse drowning in a cup of old coffee. And she thought: "I also have a hard time performing the actions that keep me alive."

One day, the woman went to the shopping district and saw a thin person walking a piglet on a leash. And she thought: "I also am bonded to people who do not understand my relationship with the world."

One day, the woman saw a sparrow opening and closing its tiny cloaca from the branches of a beech tree. And she thought: "I also make movements that have nothing to do with my situation."

XXX

No; she does not want him to come along. The woman must do it by herself. As she has said before, any empathy will be unwelcome cargo.

"But there will be details," her lover said. It is just the kind of thing he would say, at once vague and practical. Sometimes he is like a tool she does not know how to use properly, and thinking about this sends her into a splenetic bender.

"My mom used to make me clean the carpets by hand," she says.

"That sucks."

There are little things crawling under the skin of her domesticated tolerance. She has an anvil where her head should be.

"Let's get a coffee," she says.

With machine guns for eyes, the woman watches her lover's body shuffle its way up the sidewalk. His suggestion clatters around inside her throat.

What had he said? She is so angry that it is hard to remember.

This happens sometimes.

She is not kind, she is not even. Her vagina clenches in fury.

He is not the kind of person who will call her names or curse at her.

"No one is going to notice if you do the right thing," she hisses.

He doesn't engage. He is like a little dog, trapped in a car. She wants to tear a piece of flesh from his body.

But the slope of his shoulders is so sweet, as sweet as a small pink flower, so sweet that she feels love, like pain, creep in. She has become very tired. But her lover is still collecting his hurt and turning it into hostility.

She is suddenly very afraid. The woman has never learned how to fight this way. It confuses her. She has only two modes: on and off, good and bad.

"But there will be details," was all the lover had said, but of course there was a request: could he please come help her with her mother's house?

"I don't know why you want to come," she says, alight. "It's going to be sad and tedious and then it will be over."

"What if you forget something?"

"What?"

"I mean—what if you need something that you don't have, and you have to be there with her and can't leave? An extra body might be helpful."

The woman looks at his lovely face and his mouth that always retains its shape.

Rattle, rattle, rattle goes her mind, a little knot (nut!). It is faster than thought; it bounces on her tongue and forces the clumsiest kind of speech.

"It's just not possible."

"You're always going all over the place, but we're never getting anywhere," the lover says softly.

"I don't know what that means," says the woman very sincerely. That kind of restlessness belongs to thin people.

"You can be very hard."

Now she is certain he is making fun of her. Her appeal and her shame come from her softness. The lover himself likes to heft her breasts in his hands for fun.

The nut pings against the wall of her skull and sends a deep reverberation through the fatty tissue of her brain.

The woman grinds away at herself.

And then the lover is moving toward her, increasing in size. It is unbearable. She looks at his broad, even mouth, the column of his throat, his chest, his arms, the slimness of his hips, and his funny, pigeon-toed feet. He stands there radiating love and clear sight and willingness—in all things. The whites of his eyes look very clean. This goodness is nearly intolerable.

He announces again that he wants to be helpful. He shows her his hands, palms up to say, "There are no tricks here."

What a man! Is it bravery or stupidity or self-debasement? And, surely so huge that he can barely manage his task, the woman allows him to gather her into the cage of his arms.

XXXI

The old neighbor is like a die——she is always tumbling one way or another and surprising the woman with how she turns up. This is not the same as being indestructible.

Today she is vital and in excellent spirits. Today she is looking alert and healthy. She has already had her dialysis; the nursing aide has come and gone.

The woman has come over to sort the mail and to drink some bad coffee. The old neighbor cares nothing for specifics and knows only a very little bit about the woman, loves and ridicules her as any other given fact of life. Being taken for granted this way feels good. The days they see each other are elevated from the rest of the week's chaos.

The woman doesn't actually have any idea how old the old neighbor is, because she has ruined her skin with cigarettes. Today she sits like a bright child in the armchair between the window and the defunct fireplace. There are stacks of paper everywhere and framed paintings on the floor but not the walls. There are no shades in any of the windows in the living room.

"You look like you're about eleven years old, have I ever told you that?" says the old neighbor.

"Not today," says the woman. This is part of their whole routine. The ages change but never go older than twelve. Eleven means that today the woman must be wearing a particularly dour expression.

"Bring me a smoke from the kitchen?"

The woman complies because this old neighbor is not her mother. In the hall, two closed doors indicate the house's private spaces—the cramped antique bathroom and the neighbor's bedroom where the woman has only been once or twice, both times instances of extreme geriatric distress.

She finds the pack of cigarettes in their top drawer in the dark, unruly kitchen, retrieves one and a pack of matches from the jar by the stove, and returns to find the old neighbor transformed into an oracle in her armchair. The woman lights the cigarette between her own lips, drags to start the cherry, and offers it up.

The old neighbor still smokes beautifully. Like incense, stairs of blue smoke rise from her mouth and nostrils.

"Guess who died?" She looks just tickled. She smokes harder and squints at the woman through her exhalation.

"I give up."

"That young girl. The one down the street with the friendly boyfriend—struck by lightning in the country last weekend. I guess that's what you get for trying to go to a concert." The old neighbor shrugs her shoulders, waggles her eyebrows as if to say she has made another narrow escape. "The paper said the odds were one in seven hundred thousand."

The news skitters around the room along the floorboards, flits up near the battered crown molding of the ceiling, kept company by the smoke. The woman remembers this girl because they have all been residents of the cul-de-sac where the old neighbor has lived, alone, for nearly thirty years. The old neighbor still gossips purposefully about the cul-de-sac, as though neighbors and local issues had never been replaced by the Internet.

"I heard one of her eyes popped out," the old neighbor says. The woman knows she is running her countdown and that it brings her a very particular pleasure—one laced with regret—when she outlives younger people.

She has smoked for forty years and still lies about how many she has each day.

The neighbor picks up a catalogue from the arm of her chair and opens it to a dog-eared page.

"What do you think of this?" She shows the woman a model in a polyester oxford. "My daughter says I spend my money on junk. What do you think about that?"

The woman is half listening, is watching Death move on its mouse feet, on its palmetto wings, around the room. She is not frightened because dying isn't personal.

"How does that make you feel?" the woman replies, having nothing to say.

"It makes me feel like I should have taught her to mind her business."

Secondhand smoke and weak coffee have made the woman very tired so she flips slowly through her own catalogue: a series of platitudes that comprise American empathy. She looks at her favorite of the neighbor's belongings to guide her toward the right phrase.

The decorative teddy bear covered in yellowing sheepskin causes "I'm sure she means well" to take shape behind her soft palate; the box TV topped with bunny ears, which are wrapped with foil, stimulates "Have you tried talking to her about that?" somewhere in the woman's whorls of brain tissue; the plexiglass painting of Old Glory that has only forty-eight stars cues the leaden, ominous "I just think you deserve better."

But the best object is no object at all. It is the dirty sunlight coming in, made fibrous by the smoke. The woman looks at her old neighbor's tiny feet where they barely reach the floor, their fallen arches dusted with broken capillaries.

"There you are," the neighbor says. "You have on this face, and I swear to God you look like a grown-up for the first time since you moved in."

XXXII

Before the woman has a chance to ask, her pretty-necked friend confirms that yes, the dead person suffered a great deal, finally dying after four days in the hospital.

"The electrical shock made one of her eyes pop out."

"I haven't seen her in two years," says the woman. Apart from a primal flicker of unease, the parameters of her life feel exactly the same. It is sad, so sad, so sad, so sad, so sad, so sad, so sad, so sad, so sad, she thinks, trying to force herself into the appropriate mindset. But she cannot. "I have to go to a meeting," she says, and picks at a rough spot on her index finger until it becomes a proper hangnail. She bites off the little flap and pulverizes it between her front teeth. It seems to her that this is the price of surviving childhood, and then adolescence: one watches other people die or become infirm, and then one feels agitated but not surprised.

One morning, the woman had rounded the corner and there they were: the dead person and her bald boyfriend standing in front of a small apartment building. The woman was unsettled by the sight. People that she knew only vaguely through her pretty-necked friend standing there in the woman's own cul-de-sac. Being familiar. They had seemed happy to see her.

"Doesn't our door look like it's made of Swiss cheese?" the boyfriend said, and the woman realized he and the dead person had just moved in. Though she and the dog had passed the building many times, she had never noticed. But he was right. The metal door, like the cheese, was light yellow and perforated with holes of different sizes.

"I suppose it does," she said.

"You seem like you're having a perfect morning," said the dead person, reaching for her bald boyfriend's hand, and the woman could hardly believe it. They had caught her midwalk, fluctuating between terror and misunderstanding. But it was true that she made a nice picture, carrying a blue coffee cup and walking her forty-pound mutt.

"I do okay sometimes," she said.

Two weeks later, she had stood shirtless in the couple's new bedroom, the sounds of housewarming floating pleasantly through the closed door.

"That's a beautiful bra," said the dead person. "I'm sorry we don't have A/C."

"Thank you," said the woman, accepting the gray T-shirt, folding her blouse into a damp square.

"You can use some of my deodorant, too, if you want."

"Thank you," said the woman, pulling the T-shirt over her head and finding it a little too small.

After that the dead person had fixed her a plate of quiche, a coffee drink, a grapefruit and vodka. They had not spent time together again.

At that time, the woman remembers, five years ago, not two, they were compatriots: firmly arrived at adulthood with few of its material trappings and none of its security. Now the person is dead. Is the dead person closer to babyhood or to old age or to the empty paper plate in the recycling bin? The woman thinks of her mother, who must be awake by now, sitting upright in her bed at home, nauseated, or maybe pressing a palm against her sore liver, or staring angrily at the wall.

The house will soon be up for sale, and all its psychic violence and broad yellow days and the yard's dark verdure will belong to someone else. And then it might as well cease to exist altogether.

Uncomfortable, aware of her tender finger, intermittently chewing it and also tonguing the gold crown that is her favorite pacifier, the woman goes through the regulated atmosphere of her workplace to arrive at her supervisor's office on time.

"Anything fun, new, or exciting today?"

This is the supervisor's customary morning address to the employees she enjoys in spite of their shortcomings.

"Somebody I know died last night," the woman says as she sits in the appropriate chair.

"Oh my God." The supervisor leans forward, touching the hollow between her clavicles. Next to her monitor is a framed photograph of a pretty little boy in his swimming suit, smiling big, and a marble paperweight rough carved into the shape of a lotus flower. On the wall there is a framed picture of Martin Luther King, Jr., and social justice posters from an era of insincerity and naivete.

"I still have a T-shirt she lent me," she says. "Isn't that funny? It doesn't fit." In her lap, she worries at her finger, pulling away more skin until the whole fingertip is a raw, bright pink. It throbs in time with the woman's heartbeat, and she hides it in her lap.

"I don't know if I'd call it funny, exactly," says the supervisor. She peers into the woman's face. "Do you need to take time? It would be no problem."

"I didn't know her," the woman says. "Not well. Not really." She peeks down at her skirt to make sure her underwear is safely tucked away and sees that blood has filled the crack between nail and fingertip. It occurs to the woman that, today especially, she should be grateful for this vibrant color. She picks, it bleeds. "It's nothing," she says.

XXXIII

The woman cannot remember why she agreed to perform this favor, which is really a series of smaller favors under the denomination of a large one called "babysitting." She does not want a dynamic of friendship with her boss, but here she is, turning the corner and parking next to the driveway.

"Why didn't you ring the doorbell?" the boy says, answering her knock, resting a forearm on the doorjamb. Around them, the nice neighborhood is like a lifeboat floating away from the damaged ship that is the rest of the city.

"I guess I didn't think about it," she says.

"Most people ring the doorbell."

"I'll have to remember that next time."

"Why?" He smiles at her, and the woman considers that he will become a very handsome man. She tells the child her name and offers him a handshake. Like an alien, he stares at her hand before slowly clasping it with his own.

"It's nice to meet you," the woman says. "Where's your mom?"

"Putting her bra on." The boy's voice dissipates into the red sky.

Across the street, a housekeeper shakes out an intricate foreign rug. Debris tumbles into the air. The woman raises her hand in salute, trying to transmit that tonight she, too, is just the help. The other person either does not see her or pretends not to notice.

When she pulls the door closed behind her, the woman discovers it is made of aluminum.

She finds the little boy in the living room, perched on an ottoman with a clicker in each hand. Gazing at the room's beautiful decor is nearly as restful as closing her eyes. There are photos everywhere of the boy as a baby, decked in the national costume of his birth country. Many seconds pass before the woman realizes he is lowering the lights with one control and flipping channels with the other.

"It took you forever to get here," he says to the woman as his mother enters the room, clasping her necklace. Her shaven armpits look like chicken skin in the low light. Unlike the woman, her supervisor is shaped like an efficient reed. The woman wonders if she has encouraged this build in her son or if she just got lucky in selecting a baby who would grow to match her aesthetic.

"You aren't late," she says. "He just wants everything to happen as quickly as possible."

The woman refrains from saying that she relates. She also does not say it bothers her that someone so young should also have access to this compulsion.

After a lingering hug in which the woman receives a sin-cere "Thank you," her supervisor—the mother—outlines the evening schedule (homework, dinner, relaxation time, bed) and leaves.

"Can I have the tour?" says the woman.

The boy walks her through the long house, touching vari-ous objects and explaining their significance. The woman feels perverse, listening to his little boy voice, anticipating the needs of his little boy body. She wonders if he will tell her when he has to go to the bathroom, or if he will just do it. Will she need to stand outside while he goes? Will she need to remind him to wash his hands?

"We got this on vacation last year," he says, steepling his fingers over the mouth of a spindly, dove-colored vase. The woman is jealous and impressed. He shines with possibility. She cannot imagine him with acne or a job at Dairy Queen. He will move from one rarefied atmosphere to another. He will always sleep through the night.

The woman wishes his mother would have adopted her, too.

"Tell me what you like so much about it." These words shift the moment into a familiar territory. Violence whispers between them. He does not speak immediately, and she tries again in a harder voice. "Why do you like it?"

A veil of discomfort passes over the boy's bony face. "My mom says it's the best one we have."

Blinking, making a fist in her pocket, the woman remem-bers: the child is just a child. He is not inviolable. Because she feels afraid—mostly of his mother but also of her own cruelty—the woman sits on the floor at his feet and looks up at him.

"What grade are you in?"

Other avenues of conversation are closed.

"Fifth grade," he says slowly.

"I think you're a very intelligent person," she says. "Are you hungry? Maybe it's time for you to eat."

They go together into the kitchen, and she decides to fix him the kind of dinner she would have liked as a child: boxed macaroni and apple slices.

As she puts on the water and shakes the cheese packet, the boy watches her from the table. Neither of them speaks until the pasta is done.

"I think I'm supposed to have a protein, too," he says. He looks like he's about to cry, but his mother won't be home for another four hours.

"There's protein in milk. And calcium," the woman says, splashing 2 percent into the pot. The carton depicts a smiling cow with manic eyes and a bow on its head.

"My mom usually makes it with water," the boy says, so softly the woman can barely hear him. She spoons an orange mound into a white bowl. Dairy odor rises and dissipates. She salivates, swallows.

"Try it this way. If you don't like it, I'll make you something else." She sets the bowl in front of him and takes from it a forkful for herself, timing her bite with his.

"It's really good," he says. Relief spreads across his face as he chews. His little features unpinch and understanding billows into the chill of their dynamic. The sound of her food in his mouth fills the woman with satisfaction.

XXXIV

The city has turned so beautiful in its new season. From her desk, the woman can see the whole expanse of the parking lot. On the medians between parking spaces, white flowering trees fill the air with the odor of semen.

"My son's room smells like that all the time, now that he's hit puberty," says the woman's office mate.

"They're a varietal of pear tree," says the blond person nobody likes, plunging a fork into a microwavable meal.

The woman listens to this conversation but doesn't participate, cannot look away from the window, where the western sky is dark and radiant.

At home, she does sit-ups for the first time in five months and plans to meet with her most exciting, least reliable friend. While they talk she dresses for adventure in two T-shirts and a pair of shorts under a long, light coat—no bra.

As she moves from one neighborhood into the next the woman's breasts flop up and down. In an animal way her eyes and mouth feel all-black, empty, hungry for input.

She goes to the liquor store to buy a pint of whiskey.

This is not the kind of impulse she usually indulges, and it gives her the feeling that there is nothing where her brain should be.

"You look like you don't feel so good," the man says when he takes her money, and he is wrong.

The woman puts the bottle in the inner pocket of her coat where it rests hard against her left tit: a reminder of her own adventurousness. She takes a swig here and there—between a pair of parked cars, in a stinky doorway, behind a telephone pole—and the alcohol burns all the way into her empty belly. The sound of the highway drones up, and the woman feels homesick for an imagined landscape.

By the time she gets to the café, she is drunk and smiling, and the handsome staff treats her with exaggerated courtesy. She alleviates the moment by ordering an expensive drink and looking into her phone.

Though they are both nearly a half-hour late, her friend has neither called nor texted.

All the tables inside are crowded with people interacting successfully or working on their computers. Out on the patio the only empty chair is at a table occupied by a teenage boy who is so beautiful the woman is embarrassed.

She pulls her coat close around her body and asks if they might share.

"I'm waiting for my friend," she says, and though the statement is true it feels like a lie.

"I'm doing my math homework," says the boy. Up close, he looks too young to drive. His white palms flash when he turns the pages of his notebook and the woman thinks: His parents love him very much.

They sit in silence until the woman can't stand it. "My friend is insane. She probably won't show up," she says, and she and the boy laugh together as though they are friends.

Porch lights turn on up and down the street. The breeze sounds nice among the leaves but it carries a familiar bleachy stink. White petals swirl around their feet. The boy sneezes and rubs his eyes until they turn red. The woman remembers that she has allergies, too—but perhaps the liquor has taken the edge off.

"These trees smell weird, right?" says the boy.

"They're pear trees," the woman says too quickly, shifting her weight from one side of her bottom to the other. Her hands feel hot; the need to urinate spreads from her belly button to her urethra.

A skinny person of indeterminate age scoots across the street and up the sidewalk in a motorized wheelchair. There's a beer can wedged between his thighs.

"I have to go inside for a second. Need a refill?"

"I only ever drink the milk," says the boy.

She wobbles to her feet. The small bathroom smells like a barnyard because so many people have gotten piss on the floor. As she squats over the bowl and looks down, dizzy with feeling, the woman knows that's where she's going: down and under, flushed by a springtime wind.

"Why do you come here if you don't like coffee?" she says when she comes back. The streetlight dapples the boy's anxious face with patches of light like——what? Like milk, decides the woman. He must have still been on breast milk when she was in high school, maybe even college. She thinks about opening her coat to offer him a drink.

"I like being out, where other people are," he says, and something inside the woman's body contracts. She looks at the cleft above his upper lip and decides it's the same size and shape as her own fingertip.

"Me too," she says.

XXXV

The woman has not performed her back-strengthening routine because the house has no air- conditioning and the exercises make her sweat. Instead, she stays in bed, looks at the computer, and thinks about how much effort it'll take to make coffee and cook her daily egg.

The woman's oldest friend has found a sweetheart, renewed her passport, and followed him north to a colder country excluded by the woman's wireless provider. She quit her job. It has been seven weeks and nobody knows if she'll come back.

Overnight the woman's heart turned flabby with bereavement.

She knows so many people and loves so few of them.

At the end of the bed the shepherd dog vacillates between looking pathetic and licking her own vulva. The woman pushes her foot into the animal's soft belly and enjoys the feeling of an animal tongue between her toes. She puts off their walk for another hour and a half. Jealous and fearful, she cannot stop thinking about her friend.

What if her money runs out?

How can she work on a travel visa?

When will the sweetheart's divorce be finalized?

Of course, the woman understands a drive toward adventure. She herself does not want to go to work ever again. She herself is tired of dressing uncomfortably and listening to coworkers describe their lives. She herself is tired of containing institutional memory. She herself falls asleep next to her lover, thinking about trepanation.

The woman imagines her friend posing for a photo at the foot of a leaky glacier. In this fantasy, the friend makes a funny face or a peace sign, dressed in jeans and a long sweater, smiling beneath a pair of men's sunglasses.

Eventually the visualization becomes unbearable, and the woman propels her body off the bed and into the weekend world, the dog leashed at her side.

The woman and her pet pass the historical mansion that rises from a corner lot. Its roses have been on a strange schedule: blossoming and dying overnight. All of the allium stems are straw, cracking in the breeze. Some small animal has died in the grass. Viscera dots the sidewalk and the dog tries to eat it.

Even as she yanks the leash, even as the dog wheezes against her choke chain, the woman thinks of her friend.

As twenty-year-olds, they had sometimes showered together, preferring the awkward phantom of sex to the shock of being apart.

The woman remembers a lighter, or maybe a bottle cap, skittering back and forth between her friend's big hands on a picnic table.

She remembers counting condoms in her trash can after college.

She remembers learning how to buy fruit by inspecting her friend's refrigerator and pantry every season—it had turned out there was more to eating than apples.

For two years, she has tracked the development of a varicose vein behind her friend's left knee. First it was just a snaky shadow, and the woman had congratulated herself on being so observant. It transformed into a slender, complicated bulge about three inches long. If it had gotten bigger, or shown signs of thrombosis, the woman would have urged her friend to seek an outside opinion.

Then, seven weeks ago: the send-off. They had stood swallowing coffee in the driveway until the sweetheart came around the corner in his van. The woman had smiled and smiled, unable to speak, even as her friend wiped her eyes with the neck of her T-shirt.

"This is it," the friend had said.

"See you sometime," said the woman.

They hugged again, and that time the woman had not closed her eyes. Over her bony shoulder, she could see the sweetheart fiddling with his telephone in the driver's seat.

At home the woman retreats to her bedroom with a half gallon of red juice because her lover is in the kitchen making himself a snack. She takes off her shorts and shoes, eases herself to the floor, and ingests more liquid than her guts can accommodate. When the carton is empty she throws it into the hall. Her distended belly pushes her underwear past the line of her pubic hair, obscures her knees, and though she recognizes the humor in her position, it brings her no pleasure.

The woman composes a couplet of messages and presses Send:

What am I supposed to do today?
Does he know about that thing behind your knee?

Beneath the bright window the dog rests with her pink mouth closed and yellow eyes open. One ear flicks forward and back, forward and back, and swivels to attention.

XXXVI

The morning started late. The woman had lain in bed alone, listening to the sounds of insects and traffic, smelling herself in the sheets.

She needs to feed herself and the guest who will soon be arriving, but she cannot cook and her lover has left the house—"I know you like your privacy," he had said.

"Why am I such a bachelor?" the woman says to the wagging dog, whose golden eyes are round and depthless.

Within the hour her bad-lucked friend will come over for lunch, and though she is hungry, the woman does not want to ruin her own appetite. She selects a banana from the bowl by the window and eats it in three bites. She drinks a glass of water to fill up the leftover space in her stomach and pours herself a third cup of coffee.

The caffeine agitates her brain and body, and so she sets herself to cleaning the clean kitchen. Afterward she lights candles in the front room: three red tapers in the alcove and a scented votive on the coffee table. She stands back to regard her handiwork. The sweat in her armpits is cold and acrid.

Through the window, the woman watches as her friend's rickety sedan pulls up and into the driveway. On the threshold, the bad-lucked friend looks peaked, less brown than usual, and her dark hair is bundled beneath a knit cap. She has not taken much care with her appearance, and though this usually gives her an air of rakishness, today she seems young and vulnerable.

It is true that they finished college together, but the money distinction between them has grown larger with time and context.

This friend has experienced turbulence for many months, and the woman calls it "bad luck," though they both know the term is inaccurate.

Her mother lives furious and alone in an island country.

Her job disappoints her and pays poorly.

She has just undergone two expensive procedures—the first chemical, the second surgical—and her body is still very sore. The blob of tissue, she had said, was the size and shape of a blueberry when it came out in the bathtub—"That's why I thought it was all gone."

In the living room, the candles are doing their job. Only the four flames provide any light, and the woman believes this grants the room the aspect of a chapel. Her friend jabs her gently in the belly.

"What is this, a seduction scene?"

The woman understands immediately that the answer is yes: she had wanted to lure her friend toward a sense of safety.

"Are you hungry?" the woman asks.

"If I said no, we'd have to call the fucking doctor again."

The woman hides her flinch by stepping backward toward the kitchen.

"How about a turkey sandwich?"

The refrigerator stinks when she opens it, and the woman feels embarrassed.

She constructs each plate as a bulwark against the darker parts of the day, projecting a system of meaning that has always comforted her:

The wheat bread tethers her to the earth, and also the backlog of human history.

The taste of meat—slightly metallic, salty, a pink taste atop her pink tongue—reminds her that she is not alone in her body on the surface of the earth.

The cheese and mayonnaise indicate luxury, softness in their texture.

The vegetables represent character, grit, forthrightness, a willingness to take the bad with the good, to take one's lumps, chew, and swallow them, fiber and all.

For indulgence she piles a big handful of Doritos onto each plate.

"Here you go!" she says heartily. "I got these because you were coming over."

She pictures serving up the food on her knees, feeding her friend more sandwiches and chips but also broth and cool fruit. Bathing her friend's feet and hands with glycerin soap, tucking her into bed for a whole weekend, then sitting at the window and enjoying the full feeling of her house being put to good use, watching the streetlights come on and go off, awake through the night for any sound of distress.

"Lately I keep believing I'm about to have a heart attack," her friend says between bites. "But it's not like I can afford time off from work." Anger fills the high-ceilinged room, so huge and dense that it reminds the woman of a mountain range. And she knows that she will not be enough to scale it.

The woman throws a web of turkey onto the floor. Wheezing with excitement, the dog scrambles over herself to get it. Her tongue and jowls make wet, rhythmic sounds against the parquet and the women laugh at the same time.

"She's so desperate!" one of them says, and the other laughs again.

XXXVII

The woman makes herself a cup of nighttime coffee and sits at the table to do some forward-thinking.

Her lover calls these projections into the future her road trips into negative capability.

She is thinking about the night of the sale; it sounds like the title of a horror movie.

The lover still wants to come with her.

"It isn't possible," she says out loud to the empty kitchen, for practice. "I'm sorry." She knows he will not alleviate her guilt by looking relieved.

She must go, again, alone, all those miles to make the sale happen.

All the good furniture will be sold. The absolute necessities (bed, couch, table, one chair) will go to the efficiency apartment. The arrow-patterned china will be gone. Most of the jewelry: gone. The art and the decorative ceramics and five of the six handwoven rugs: gone.

Illness is plain and expensive.

The woman will take only what would otherwise end

up being trash. And some clothing as well, like all the belts and big sweaters that are old enough to be fashionable again; knicknacks from side tables and windowsills. She looks around the little kitchen. Where will everything go? There are only two closets, and one of them is filled with coats. There is no basement, the attic is sealed, and the crawl space under the porch is suitable only for spiders and the occasional neighborhood cat.

The woman pours herself another mug of coffee and takes it to the stoop so she can drink it and watch telephone wires parse the sunset. The shapes of irrational totems from her childhood—a favorite doorknob, a rhombus of sunlight on the floor of the dining room, the soles of her mother's best pumps—float among the evening clouds.

The woman has already decided she and her mother will stay that first night in the motel on the way out of town, where, as a child, the woman had always wanted to play in the kidney-shaped pool. Her negative capability carries her forward into their room with its two double beds and to the new child she does not want. The new child who is her mother.

The wallpaper behind their headboards will depict a forest glade in sepia.

"That kind of forest doesn't exist in this part of the country," the woman will say, making conversation from her position near the door. She will be in the midst of making a courteous exit to retrieve their dinner from the second-best of four pizza places in town.

"I think it's pretty." Her mother will put her long, dry hand on the trunk of one of the maples. The light from the table lamp will smooth out her face, and she will look about six years old.

"You're right."

It will be a summer evening, regardless of the season, and the woman will have rolled down all the windows on her way back from the restaurant. The breeze will smell like fertilizer and, because this is a fantasy, rain. She will have both sets of keys and that will be the saddest detail. The pie will be congealing in its cardboard box, but she will take the long way toward the motel to see the soy fields, green and fertilized. The sagging barn. The imaginary interstices between "town" and "country."

Of course, this drive, this cavalcade of bereavement, will take her back to the house. The woman will not know how she arrived, but every inch of pavement and gravel will have directed her there.

She will enter it as her mother once did, however many years ago, and see it empty.

The house without its furnishings will feel much smaller than the woman is used to. She will go room to room. She will not remember any personal or domestic milestones because her mind has never worked properly in that respect: she is an adult child who meanders from one impression to the next.

She will look through all the drawers in the kitchen, and will leave the black ballpoint pen and few coins—say, a penny and three dimes—that she finds at the bottom of the one beneath the telephone station. There will be light in the kitchen windows, but the night will be developing, and the woman will feel her eyes adjusting to the dark. She will pause to rest her cheek against the living room wall, as though it were the flank of a trusted animal. It will be cool and tremorless. She will feel so old after a lifetime of feeling so young.

Being there will be quiet but it will not be silent. There will be the old neighborhood sounds with no upholstery or house linens to absorb them. The woman will become the stranger in the house, who says her own name softly in the dark.

XXXVIII

The sports bra wrangles her breasts into a tidy, forgettable loaf.

The map on the old T-shirt outlines a wild archipelago the woman will never visit.

The satin turtleneck provides an objective measure by which to monitor the changes in her physical stature.

The oversized jeans turn her into a man, except in the reflections from mirrors and street-facing windows.

The old brown belt turns her into a mother from a bygone decade, resolutely addicted to cough syrup.

XXXIX

The jet arcs over the plains, carrying the woman toward her family obligation. The closer she gets to her native geography the more raw and humane she becomes.

Currently, everything hurts and feels good at the same time. She, a human animal, was never meant to travel so quickly.

The woman interprets the interior of the plane as a vast, communal living room.

Right before takeoff, a young man in a cropped Capote coat had sauntered toward her down the aisle. His khaki-colored hair swept back toward his crown. The woman drew herself up taller in her seat, prepared to make conversation. But he had swung into row seven and the passenger walking behind him—effortlessly limbed, chic even in sweatpants—folded herself into the same compartment. When she pulled a handful of natural hair out of her collar and pushed the curls over her shoulder, the woman could smell her perfume.

"Yeah, babe, you're right as per usual," said this other, beautiful passenger. "But the point is that I didn't know that

I didn't know those things. So how could I have done differently?" And the passenger leaned over to kiss the handsome man with her whole mouth.

Hearing an admission of such a human foible from someone so glamorous, the woman decided she adored them both.

Now, twenty thousand feet over the surface of the earth, instead of reading her book, she watches them cuddle and share a water bottle. From behind, she can almost believe their cheekbones convey a moral message. It is obvious they have money, but it doesn't matter whether it is earned or inherited; their grace remains the same.

After a while they settle down into a single shape, sharing a long gray scarf like a blanket.

It's only thirty minutes from touchdown and they still haven't moved. The woman retrieves two mandarins from her carry-on, peels and eats them both, swallowing the seeds, thinking of her lover's small teeth and predictable sense of humor. Her phone contains a message in which he bids her a safe flight, as though this courtesy could prevent a plane crash.

Staring at the couple in row seven, the woman considers that such a finale might be the best way to go. The least-lonely option. A surge of filial love warms the inside of her body. She thinks about the community the three of them might make among themselves, if only they knew she was there, behind them, brimming. She imagines touching their bodies as the plane tumbles out of its trajectory, the imminence of death obliterating the personal boundaries that have always stymied and disappointed her.

She'd tell them: "I very much believe in God, but only when things are going bad for me," and afterward her heart would be light. Her new companions would nod, thrust beyond language by the extremity of the situation, grateful for her honesty. The beautiful passenger might smooth the hair away from her temples, or push a tear away from the bridge of her nose. The woman thinks of their arms around her amidst the noise, the rushing air, the alarms, the nausea, the crying, the ugliness in everyone's face.

Her row mate, a fat person whose elbow has colonized the armrest for an hour, does not factor into this fantasy.

The peels have become sticky in the woman's fist, but she can't drop them onto the floor and won't allow herself to hide them in the chair pocket at her knees. The barf bag is long gone; she needs a trash can.

She decides to take her refuse to the bathroom in order to walk past the couple, to force them, gently, to contend with her presence as she has contended with theirs. To know for certain if she could ever belong to their little family, if only for the duration of the crash.

Upon standing, however, she can see their eyes are closed. She sits back down.

Looking out the porthole window, the woman believes she can comprehend the vastness of the North American continent. Frontage roads parcel the winter farmland into squares, where thicker lines indicate an occasional highway, all of it bound by a single unknown county.

When she looks up, the couple in row seven has shifted positions. She can see their hands again. The man's wedding ring—big, custom-made—glitters in the overhead light. The woman takes a photograph of it on her phone.

The voice, when it comes to her, resonates with the round tones of her own heritage.

"Cute, aren't they?"

"I'm sorry?"

"It's nice, right? Seeing a happy couple. It's a rare thing, anymore."

"What?"

"Would you like something to drink? Coffee, tea, pop?" This final word strikes her. Pop. Pop!

"I have these." Her voice cracks, and she shows the flight attendant her sticky handful.

"I'm sorry, hon, I'm only doing beverage service right now," he says. Wrinkles frame his mouth and deepen when he smiles. The skin along his jaw looks loose, like her mother's. Is he laughing at her? She wants to touch his hand, explain herself and the photo, but says instead, "Well, I'll be here when you come back."

XL

The woman goes throbbing on the interstate in her rental car. She goes throbbing past the bad tidings of the foreclosed farm. She goes throbbing up Main Street. She goes throbbing to her mother's house, passing her father's place along the way.

It is either a bad coincidence or a case of providential humor that the stoppage of her medicine coincided with this visit. Cue nausea, diarrhea, and a constant electric, internal vibration that loosens her mind.

As she exits the car, someone drives by and waves and the woman makes herself dizzy by waving back. Everything appears very far away and very sharp, as though she were looking through the wrong end of a telescope. The woman burps up a mouthful of sour foam and spits it onto the curb.

The sky is dark and the weather is warm. The woman agrees with her mother: it seems like it will never snow again.

The house contains the long, yellow days of the woman's childhood and adolescence, and she enters it without knocking. Evening shadows have crept across the pine floors her mother installed over a series of weekends, years and years ago.

The mother appears in the hall, wiping her hands on a dish towel. Her hair is wild in the way she likes and she has gotten very thin. Seeing this, the woman would like to go up to her old bedroom, close the shades, and sleep for a week.

"I'll leave my stuff on the porch until I can wipe the dog hair off," she says.

"Just throw it anywhere you want," says her mother. "And give your old mom a hug!"

Caught wholly off guard, the woman accepts her mother's diminished body into her arms.

Her mother has no health insurance and no credit cards. She has been paying for her treatment and medicines out of pocket, and she has doctor friends who help her with samples and after-hours clinic visits whenever there is a gap. The family money has been gone for a long time, though the woman went to good schools with no debt and her mother still has expensive dinnerware in all the cupboards.

As they cook dinner and set the table with this dinnerware, the woman's mother talks.

She would like to get a roommate to pay off her second mortgage. She is on another diet and, as an investment, will soon buy a used luxury car. The man at the garage has a near-mint sedan and said he would hold it for thirty days. She will not go on a date with him, though he would be sexy if he ever fixed his teeth.

They are halfway through their meal and it has become obvious that life has no definite shape. The woman watches her mother compose a bite of chicken and maneuver it into her mouth. The fork emerges and the woman thinks, I was also once surrounded by that body. Then, feeling very thirsty, she thinks, This visit is different.

"Why do you have that face on?" says her mother, spooning more mixed vegetables onto the woman's plate. There's a hair floating on the upper disk of her water but the woman gulps it down anyway, spilling a little out of the corner of her mouth. She takes off her sweatshirt and uses it to wipe her lips and then her brow.

She is about to burn right up.

"No face," she says and goes to open the dining room window. Her palm fogs up the glass. It is January and it is night, but there are birds singing at the feeder.

Her grasp on the moment seems untenable.

"I could use a cup of coffee," says her mother cheerfully. "You?"

"I can't have caffeine this late."

"You've been sensitive since you came out. This much I know for sure."

The woman perks up. A fight would be a relief. "I'm not sensitive," she says. "Just ill."

"Well, you know me—I never met a habit I didn't like." The mother chuckles as she pushes away from the table and goes into the kitchen.

While her mother makes the coffee, the woman marches to the bathroom and inspects the medicine cabinet, the linen closet, and the toilet tank. She discovers nothing except that the bathroom is spotless.

They do the dinner cleanup in silence until the mother reveals a secret.

"I got us some cupcakes," she whispers, and the woman bursts into tears.

Once she's dried herself out, they eat the cupcakes while watching a celebrity gossip show on the little brown TV set with the convex screen. Framed above it is a new decoration, a retro cross-stitch in pink and white that reads: MAKE IT DO. WEAR IT OUT. USE IT UP. DO WITHOUT.

The woman licks the last of the bottle green frosting off her plate. She turns to ask where the cross-stitch came from, but her mother has fallen asleep with her mouth wide open. Gazing at the brown bits of cake in her molars, the woman thinks, I will always be surrounded by that body, and a familiar electricity zigzags down from her brain and through both arms.

Moths have laid eggs in the pantry and there is hair collecting in the fridge.

XLI

The woman goes to get the paper and her breath steams in the cold air. The threat—the promise—of a real winter has risen with the sun.

She knows different houses hew, affectively, toward different seasons. This one, her mother's house, is a summer house. Even in a blizzard it feels breezy and light. A guest once said it had the feeling of a pavilion.

Her father's is a winter house, stitched up against the cold and bolstered with fabric and rich food.

The house the woman shares with her lover is a spring house, a chipper little place doing its best as it pushes through the days like a crocus through snow.

Her neighbor's house is an autumn house, and not because the neighbor's age means the place is proximate to death. No—it's the artifacts, talismans of a fading world that hasn't quite disappeared.

In the living room, the woman's mother is eating a green apple in the armchair by the bay window. She hands it over to the woman, her daughter.

"I think a good Granny Smith is one of my favorite foods," says the mother. "And a rare steak." But her voice is filled with chagrin. "Can't eat that anymore, that's for sure."

The apple's floral smell turns the room into a garden. Blood streaks its white flesh.

"Your gums are bleeding again," the woman says, and pivots the piece of fruit so her mother can see.

"You'd better not," says her mother.

"I guess I'd better not." The woman returns the apple so her mother can take another bite.

"It's the medicine," she says with her mouth full. "Look at what it's done to my fingernails. They grow so fast now." It is true; they are much longer than usual and excellently almond shaped.

"You should paint them," says the woman. Being her mother's daughter has taught the woman that the body is horror waiting to happen. And it has come true: there is an infection in the blood. "Burgundy would be good on you."

"Interferon chic," says her mother, and the woman laughs. It is rare that her mother is empathetic enough to be clever. "I've been thinking about your stepdad a lot lately," the mother says. "He was handsome. I always told him he could have done catalogues or something. Except for his teeth."

The woman's mother has not mentioned this man for a long time. He had been a decent, sad person without much money, his son handsome and unwell. The rush of cold masculinity, these two male people showing up like cowboys, the smell of testosterone. Their arrival turned her life into a narrative that she could look at from the outside in. The marriage had been short and the divorce bad.

Her mother has been single ever since. The woman considers her mother's sexual appeal, which had always seemed monstrous. A quotation from some book, some movie, a whole lifetime, a whole narrative ago: "The most attractive people always remind us of big cats." The mother—one long leg folded beneath her and the other one hooked over her thigh—is rotating her foot in the air. Her long, aristocratic toes and their mangled nails, thick from years of abuse.

The summer feeling doesn't come from the house but from her mother. And this is part of her attractiveness. The promise of a special experience. The woman's mother is an ouroboros of threat and promise.

But she is a sick person slowly eating her apple. And now she is complaining like someone her age about the weather and the draft coming in through the casement. The woman brings her a white blanket with tassels like roses, to warm her and to cover the sight of all the bones in her chest.

XLII

Tonight the woman will open the book for the first time in her adult life.

A paperback that has never gone out of print, the book drew her through puberty, and she had been relieved to find it. Then twelve, she had been sleeping poorly because of the streetlight in her window. The locust trees in the yard had just come into flower. She had developed neither her breasts nor her mustache but was ripe for obsession.

She brought the book to school and to the grocery store and to the movies, finished all 803 pages in five days. She read it again, then read it again.

"You carry that thing around because you want everyone to see you reading such a big book," said her mother.

Except for a figure with wild hair, the title in bold red letters, and "1987" inscribed in the artist's tiny handwriting, the cover is white. Now the volume sits in two halves on the bottom of her bookshelf, communicating:

Stasis and pursuit.

Illness and desire.

Mystery and revelation.

Its spine had always been weak. As a child, the woman believed she would eat it when it finally fell apart.

Tonight she enters the living room and picks up the book with both hands. Its plastic-lined cover flakes beneath her fingers. She feels afraid because she knows the text won't hold up. Years have passed and her tastes have changed. She no longer finds it romantic to imagine the end of the world.

But there on the first page is the brown fingerprint, her own adolescent scrawl—

book belongs to ME.

—written in blood from a sore on her head.

She opens the door onto her side yard and all the windows. Potential whispers among the leaves, stifling her adulthood in a way that feels good.

As the woman turns them, the pages fall out of their binding.

The antihero—a blond—hovers between archetype and cliché. She had fallen in love with him.

He makes his appearance on page 17 riding a *red pony*, wearing a *dark poncho*. Eternally twenty-four. He says *I have no money*, having fled a bad deal in a dead city, leaving his lover behind. He is the trickster in a trash mythology and the center of its universe.

He travels.

On page 29 he seduces the son of his friendly host and whisks him into the desert.

The woman remembers: after reading this passage she had gone into the family bathroom, taken off all her clothes, and grieved her feminine body.

On page 116, the boy is killed.

The woman had cried for them, then retrieved a pair of scissors from the nighttime kitchen and given herself a bad haircut.

On page 288, berserk with grief, the hero murders his oldest friend.

The woman had gone into the basement and explored her stepbrother's hidden cache of pornography.

On page 334, the hero enters a farming town surrounded by hills. For three years, people love him in the ways that they know how, but civil war forces him to leave.

The woman had prayed for him while touching the inside of her nose and picking the scab on her head, then wiped her fingers along the white margins.

Time compacts his grief and guilt into something hard and dark inside him. He wanders *yet another countryside*, drunk, trailing emotional soot, until the end, pages 769 through 803, wherein he peels back the mystery of his nature—good as well as bad—and ascends to a position of power in a vast and radiant city.

The woman had closed the book and gone barefoot into the yard to listen to cars on the boulevard, and when joy and bereavement had twisted her bowels, she farted painfully among the roses.

Tonight her old love rises from its hiding hole.

She still looks for his *sensitive hands* and *violet eyes* among the bodies of strange men and boys. Maybe if she looks hard enough now—there, in the western corner of the room, between the bookcase and the couch—she could see him sitting on the floor, *legs crossed at the ankles.*

"I missed you." She says the words out loud and pretends her voice is his. The woman is herself but she has been him, too, for eighteen years.

XLIII

They have driven across the man-made creek through different, low-lying neighborhoods, the city park, and a gravel lot to arrive at this flower store where the woman spends more money on her party. She selects hollyhock and fountain grass because today her taste is wild.

When she tells the shop owner it is her milestone birthday, he strips a rose of its thorns and hands it to her but does not take any money off the total.

In the parking row, a young stranger regards the flowers. Sunlight bounces off her short, bright hair, and she proclaims the bouquets beautiful.

"What if nobody comes?" the woman says to her lover as he arranges himself in the passenger's seat. The bouquets crisscross his lap, and the concentrated sunlight of the windshield illuminates all the gold in his dark hair.

Sometimes the woman loves him so much she would like to chew on his nail clippings.

Sometimes she loves him so much she craves the body of someone, anyone, else.

"You're a whiner," he says, and she drives them home to the little house on the cul-de-sac.

In the kitchen, he splits the bouquets into smaller, devotional bundles, and helps the woman arrange them, plus candles, in each window. Afterward they fill the bathtub with ice, champagne, and cheap beer, and he urinates while the woman darkens her eyebrows. In the mirror, she watches his penis appear and disappear inside the brown pants.

"Thank you for your help today," she says.

Fifteen minutes before the appointed hour the woman opens all the doors and windows. The hot day has conceded to a humid, resonant dusk, and she wants to capture some of that feeling inside the house.

Nighttime arrives and headlights move across the lawn.

Someone's semiprecious pendant juts hard and blue into the woman's sternum when they embrace.

"I couldn't believe this was your house when I pulled up," says this person in her pretty voice, meaning that from the street, the house is a flotilla of lanterns and that she had not anticipated such beauty from the woman's party.

"Yeah? How come?" The woman's nerves might dance out of her skin.

"What can I get you to drink?" says her lover. As usual, the world organizes itself according to his decency: the guest tells him what she wants, he retrieves it, and the path to conflict disappears.

The night develops and the party exceeds its potential. There is ash all over the floor because everyone is smoking. Bodies spurt through the open door and onto the porch, where everyone speaks very loudly. The woman's good friends are all here, standing together like a chorus: the suffering but wild, returned from the north; the arch and brittle and brilliant; the red-tufted Hercules, with his competence and insensitivity. They are speaking together, enjoying each other. How incredible, how truly divine that there are three of them! Who are all these other people, and why does she need any of them?

But between the dish rack and the dining table in the tiny kitchen, a tall acquaintance illustrates his conversation by wagging his finger. Their previous encounters have taught the woman that his humor requires a taste for cruelty, and, seeing him again, hearing his voice, the woman becomes very aware of her tongue in her mouth.

"I've never seen someone work so hard for something in my entire life," says the acquaintance. He is talking about an old friend who developed early onset diabetes.

The woman knows her lover would think poorly of her for laughing. From across the kitchen, his black eyes look very forthright in his white face. Didn't he encourage her to have this party? "It's nice to see you," says the acquaintance from within his fine dark shirt. Behind him, the world is leaking in through the open windows and open door. All the candles have burned out, and the only illumination comes from the street lights and the moon. Looking from the handsome acquaintance to the wagging heads of her other guests and back again, the woman thinks, What a success.

"I'm glad you could come," she says. Her mouth is thick with alcohol.

"Happy birthday." They embrace, and when his hot, clean breath flushes her ear, all she can think is that he is mean and handsome. This has always been her favorite combination and remembering it fills her with grief.

The woman presses herself against the hall wall and slumps to the floor.

"I didn't know it was that time already," he says and sits down next to her. The hardness and warmth of his thigh against hers flood her body like a narcotic. Ready for sexual labor, she would like to push her face into his armpit. The woman looks down; she's wearing one mule and the other is wedged awkwardly beneath her ankle.

Blinking slowly, breathing through her sour mouth, she looks for her lover among the shadows in the dim kitchen. As soon as she asks, he will send all these people away and tuck her into the bed where they will not have sex, and where she will fall asleep bolstered by his good intentions.

The woman finds him at the door with moonlight on his face and a lapis pendant clutched in one hand. He is tugging it gently, playfully—the chain is still looped around someone's neck. From her position on the floor the woman can see only a corresponding mass of shadow and hair and the wink of a cocktail glass. She would like to speak with her lover, urgently, but cannot remember why. Never more handsome, never more beloved, he is smiling so hard she thinks he must have caught a star between his teeth.

XLIV

There is a jar of red marbles irradiating the bedroom windowsill.

There is a fleece of golden bitch dozing near the door.

There is a scaffold of white lover cooking in the downstairs kitchen.

There is a mound of yellow blanket softening the house's only bed.

There is a bowl of green apples ripening on the table.

There is a pair of silver tweezers glittering on the countertop.

There is a bar of transparent soap smearing the bathroom sink.

There is a basket of contentment in one room that becomes a lattice of constraint in the other.

XLV

It is very early but it is not still dark outside. The broad yellow floor boards are slashed with light, and the child feels for warmth with her toes. Her eyes are still wonky with the desire for more sleep, but her mother has gotten her up for a reason and is holding open the front door, bracing it with her foot. Her hands are full of the mugs she is carrying.

They go onto the front porch. There is an air of occasion, like a holiday, or a snow day, or a day when the child gets to leave school early to travel or go to the doctor.

"I thought we could have a coffee date this morning," says the mother. One mug—the child's favorite—is a pink so pale it is almost white, with a handle that is a perfect half circle. The child leans forward to grasp it with both cold hands and discovers that it is full of hot milk. Her mother takes it back and lifts her own mug, a camping relic made of tin, and pours a dark stream of coffee into the milk.

"Do I have school?" The child sips the tan concoction, expecting it to taste like caramel. She has only had coffee two or three times before, and then only a sip each time. She does not like the taste, but she likes the feeling of drinking it.

"It's Tuesday!" The mother laughs so the child does, too, and pushes her feet into a drift of dried leaves. Light winks in the frosted grass. "Oh yes, of course you do," the mother says. "Yes." She closes her eyes in pleasure and loosens her robe to expose the skin of her throat to the sunlight. Heedless of the chill.

Years later, the child will remember her mother in terms of her wild female masculinity, and the various chemical cravings that shorten both her attention span and her life, but right now the mother is just a mother in slippers and a pilled robe.

"I wanted to talk to you about something very important," says the mother. "How often do you think about God?"

The child has no language to put around her answer. She thinks about a globular, diaphanous pink in the sky—a big cloud, with a secretive, smiling face that looks happy and sad at the same time.

A big pressure comes down out of the air around her head. It pushes down; it enters her skull through her eye sockets. She yawns.

"I know—I woke you up a little extra early this morning. But this is really important. This is something I've been learning about, and I wanted to share it with you."

The mother tells her child that someone has taught her the most important piece of information in the world.

"God is real," she says, beaming. The sun is in her face

but she does not shade her eyes with her hand. She doesn't even appear to blink. It is like she is becoming the sun. It is contained in her dense hair, her high brow, the bridge of her Aryan nose. Finally, the child comes to understand that she is expected to respond.

"That's really cool," she says.

Her mother corrects her: "It's more than cool. It's everything."

The child knows that different adults have their different gods—she has learned about this in school, and her father is Jewish, which means that some people can't pronounce her last name correctly and also means that he believes in one fewer god than most people do, though of course he never talks to her about it.

The mother tells the child more. She says again that God is real, but the miracle is that God can look different for everyone, which is appropriate, because not everyone is the same.

She says it again. "It's really more appropriate. Because different people need different things."

"Yep," says the child.

"What do you need?"

Sometimes the mother asks questions in this manner—like she's addressing a third, older person who has a capacity to think quickly and respond in kind. The child has the urge to turn and look around, in case someone else has joined them. As usual, she cannot speak.

The mother sighs deeply and puts her mug down on the step at her feet. "It's almost time for you to get your stuff together, but let's try praying before we start our day." She takes the child's hands in her own, which are cold and hard and very dry. She closes her eyes.

The child closes her eyes, too, and looks at the matte darkness there, lit up in places by the sun, as though she were looking out from inside of an egg. The sunspots are the same pink as that benign, happy-sad face, and the child can see it swiveling to look at her. Its eyes are dots.

Inside, the child is opaque.

Her mother says round-sounding words. The child wonders if the neighbors can see them, sitting here like the morning isn't about to escape and leave them scrambling to catch up.

"I think my higher power looks like a big cat, like a lion. A black one, with red eyes," the child says when her mother is finished speaking to God. The child is not lying. Rather, this is the image she wishes would come to mind when she thought of God. She wants God to be something excellent. Something powerful and impressive. She is sure she has given a good answer.

"You don't have to tell me about it," says her mother. "It should be private."

The birds, who have been awake for a long time already, seem to take up this refrain, and the child hears their exchange quavering in the treetops:

It should be private.

Did you hear?

It should be private.

Did you hear?

It should be private.

Acknowledgments

Endless thanks to my agent, Kiele Raymond, who's seen this book in all its configurations and has known just what to do with every one of them. Thank you to my editor, Athena Bryan, for your conscientiousness and precision— and patience. Thanks to Valerie and Dennis and everyone at Melville House for taking this manuscript and turning it into a bona fide book! Special thanks to Raluca Albu, Leah Dworkin and Liza St. James for endless support and constant conversation. Same goes to Will Augerot, Kyle Sturgeon, Katrine Jensen, Bonnie Chau, Sarah Harvey, Sam Clegg and Heather Radke. Also thank you to Talia Curtis and the White Review, and of course to Paul Beatty, Sam Lipsyte, Ben Marcus and Leslie Jamison, who helped me remember that feeling is thinking is writing. Wild love and gratitude to my oldest, best friends Justin Burnell, Hannah Sunshine, Emily McCabe Carter, Dakota Moe, Katy Jane Tull, Nick Shapiro, Breonne DeDecker, Jocine Velasco, Angela Lawson, Erin McBurney, and the whole Ring Family (Mandy,

Ringo, Lyda and Frankie). Thanks to recent friends who feel like old friends—Margaret Roberts, Kylie Gava, Nicole Novak, and Ethan Forsgren. To all my parents: Joey, Jody, and Janie, and to the sibs Cadiz, Rachel and sweet Theo. Thank you, thank you.

A Note About the Author

Ari Braverman is the winner of the 2012 James Knudsen Prize in Fiction and a finalist for the 2017 White Review Short Story Prize. Her work has appeared in leading literary journals including *Guernica* and *Bomb*.